The Silent Song

Life and Death and
"What is Meant to Be"

Rod Hacking

Copyright © 2024   Rod Hacking

All Rights Reserved

ISBN: 9798334329102
Independently published

In Thanksgiving for

BISHOP JEREMY TAYLOR

(1613 – 1667)

Author of Holy Living and Holy Dying

A memorial in Exeter Cathedral:

Sacred
to the memory of SARAH PRICE CLARKE, who was the only surviving issue and heiress of GODFREY CLARKE Esq of Sutton Hall in the County of Derby.
She departed this life in the city of Exeter on the 24th of November 1801.
In her were united all the virtues
which give dignity to birth, or utility to fortune.
Her mind possessed an energy
which does not often mark the female character
Her friendship was warm, and her charity was never restrained by individual convenience.
Her bosom was the seat of those energies which give activity to virtue.
Possessed of superior talents and unimpeached honour, she never pursued frivolity with severity, or the loss of fame with triumph.
Her latter years were marked by declining health, /and her sufferings by patience.
Her faith was fervent, her reward is sure.

With love and huge gratitude to my soul friend Robert Gussman for all his corrections and suggestions. The remaining faults are of course my own.

North Berwick

Berwick-upon-Tweed is the northernmost place in England (so much so that the football team plays in the Scottish leagues!) and when I say I come from North Berwick those who don't know better wonder if, despite my obvious accent, I'm really English! But the two places are 39 miles apart and North Berwick is north even of Edinburgh geographically. It is a town on the coast where the Firth of Forth meets the North Sea, and if you grow up and live there you quickly get used to the cold winds which blow from the Urals even in summer. It's a great place for golfers and seeing seabirds and I am so glad to be able to have had it as my home. My mum and dad, Ken and Laura, still live there.

For the first years of my life, I was Elizabeth McKenzie (Lizzie to my family and friends). It's long been common for women to change their surnames on marriage but for quite some time now I have been Bahuputtika Soṇā, and this is the story of how this came about and how it is that I now live in the Yorkshire Dales where, though still Soṇā, I'm mostly known as Lizzie by the locals.

I was the third child and appeared nine years after the second, and though I love my brother and sister there is quite an age gap between us. My dad was a draughtsman and my mother a nurse, so you would think they could have done their planning more successfully, but I grew up in a family in which I knew only love, security and a great deal of laughter. After Primary School in the town I went to Preston Lodge High School, a 20-minute train ride away and as I was the only one who made this journey from home, I quickly developed the habit of reading with great concentration each morning and afternoon, a skill I still enjoy, no matter what is going on around me. I read a great deal on those train journeys, which served me well when it came to Highers and University, where I would eventually study English literature for four years – what a privilege, even though I must confess that my preferences were for English writers rather than Scottish!

In retrospect I can see how my later life was shaped by my constant habit of going out to sit by myself looking out at the sea, sometimes for up to half an hour at a time. Mum and dad might have thought this odd but never said so, always allowing my siblings and myself support in whatever we might choose for our lives.

Living away from my school in Prestonpans I did not have close friends with whom I spent non-school time, and friends I did have in North Berwick from Primary School drifted away once I was at another school. I never minded this, and by now my brother and sister had already left home, but I have always enjoyed my own company which is what would later enable me to spend long periods in isolation. But that is to jump ahead.

As I approached Highers at the age of 17 with the near certainty of a place at University, I decided to take advantage of an opportunity I learned from a boy who had left school two years before me. He had come back to the school to tell the story of how he had been selected to spend 12 months with another boy of his own age in Honduras. His enthusiasm for what he described excited me and after talking it over with my parents, I applied to *Project Trust*, an organisation based in the unlikely setting of the Isle of Coll, an island off the West Coast of Scotland. Simply getting there is an adventure, requiring eventually, three trips via a slow train journey from Glasgow to Oban, and a 2½ hour boat trip to Tiree and Coll. The joke was that if you could survive the boat without being sick you were automatically accepted, but in practice the week-long selection process was demanding, which if an applicant was coming from Cornwall or Kent, was a massive undertaking. If an applicant struggled with this, how would they manage in a far-off land with possibly only one other person who spoke English.

I have been nothing if not single-minded all my life and I was determined to win acceptance and it was a great day when my notification arrived though it then meant a longer stay on Coll, which was no hardship. I adored the emptiness of the beaches, and knew it was only a few miles from the Isle of Iona on which early Christian missionaries settled from Ireland, which is sometimes called a "thin place", meaning the proximity of heaven can almost be felt. I never visited Iona but on Coll I felt something similar. And then came the incredible news that a girl called Naomi and I were being paired and sent to Nepal!

On family holidays I had visited Spain, France and Italy so I used to being in lands where culture was different, something I had always enjoyed, preferring out of the way places to the big cities and resorts, but the prospect of Kathmandu was something else especially as our combined Nepalese was non-existent, though Naomi, from Bala in North Wales, was fluent in Welsh and said she would try that if ever her English failed to communicate. But the poor children to whom we were being sent as teachers of English were to acquire it through Welsh and Scottish accents!

We flew out from Manchester, for me an easy flight from Edinburgh, and for Naomi and her parents a relatively straightforward car journey to their nearest airport. We left on what was a cool September afternoon, via Dubai, and arrived in a very hot Kathmandu at 8:00 in the morning. There then followed the sort of bus journey that might be described as hair-raising but only as an understatement!

We were heading for Hilepani, a small town accessible only by the Mid-Hill Highway but this was no motorway akin to anything we had ever known and making the sea crossing to Coll on a stormy day seem like a piece of cake! As we made the bus journey, Naomi and I realised that we had been selected because of our familiarity with the mountains of Snowdonia and the Highlands, but nothing had prepared us for this, and from time to time as we journeyed we caught a glimpse of the mighty Himalayas to the north.

The town is about 100 miles from Kathmandu, but with regular stops en route, it still took six hours. For some of the time we followed the twisting course of the Sunkoshi River and at one point stopped for a food break at the Hotel Peace Haven, where I think we would have been quite happy to take advantage of what its title claimed to offer. But then we climbed from the river into the hills to our home for the next eleven months, the altitude of which was just over 5,000 ft., higher than both Ben Nevis and Snowdon by almost 1,000 ft. This was going to take some adjusting to.

We knew we would be being met at the bus station by a woman called Hanka (pronounced Henka), and there she was waiting with a welcoming smile and her three children who were clearly excited by the prospect of two exhausted and slightly bewildered young women.

Hanka had what once might have been a Jeep but had been added to, enabling transportation for family, friends and their luggage. Both Naomi and I would soon be using it to get around, though at home we had both only recently passed our driving tests. Our home for the year was a comfortable wooden structure which we feared would be very cold when the winter arrived, but which had a kitchen, a proper loo (what a welcome sight that was given our anticipatory fears!) which flushed from time to time, and two beds, plus a living and working section with a desk and some chairs. There was even a television which featured mostly

Nepalese programmes but some American with Nepalese subtitles. Some were extremely dated and in black and white.

There was no obvious husband/father in Hanka's house and on our first evening she had prepared for us what we would soon know as Dal, Bharat, Ra Tarkari, (dhal, rice and vegetable curry) as we would be eating it most days, though sometimes for special occasions there was Ghorkali Lamb, a variation on the theme of curry, but unbelievably tasty.

For our first two days, apart from regular visits from Hanka's three children, all under 10, we tried to sleep as much as possible and adjust to the altitude. Hanka also drove us through the town and showed us where in a few days we would begin to teach, but also, and to both our surprise and delight, an internet café which we were able to use to let our parents know how we had settled. We would soon see it much used by the many trekkers who changed buses here before heading north towards Everest.

By our western standards the town was very poor and even without any architectural knowledge we could see buildings which we thought would provide little protection if for example, there was an earthquake (as of course there was in 2015 which killed 9,000 people, albeit the worst effects were felt in Kathmandu itself, though, as we learned, an aftershock 17 days after the initial quake, had more of an effect on Hilepani, bringing down many homes and other buildings and causing injuries to many, though it seems no one in the town lost their lives. There was no hospital in the town but there was something called a Health Post not too far away. We had come equipped with all sorts of medications though never needed to seek medical assistance.

We would each be working half-time at the Shree Mahadevsthan Secondary School but also assisting the English teacher in the Shree New Star English Boarding School which was close to where we lived. With our accents the English teacher (himself Nepalese) had difficulty understanding us, so how he hoped we might be able to manage conversation classes with the old children we were somewhat unsure of as we began, when of course we had no Nepalese, though within three months we were both able to communicate satisfactorily (well, to our own satisfaction!).

On the day before we began the work we had come to do, Hanka drove us north to Manebhanjyang and beyond to allow us a view of Everest, or Sagarmāthā, the goddess of the sky, as it is known in Nepalese. I had of course seen many photographs, but nothing could prepare me for the sight of these towering peaks, which reduced me to silence and wonder.

Those trekking to Everest often came through Hilepani on their way towards the Himalayas but mostly only transferred from one bus to another and did not help the local economy, though more than a few broke their journey at the Prabash Hotel and Restaurant a few miles up the Harkapur-Okhalddhunga Road to sample more westernised food. On this day before we began work, Hanka stopped there on our way back and we indulged with burgers and fries! Shame on us! But wonderful!

Now we had to settle down and begin what we had come to do, to try and teach English to children from 10 to 16, boys and girls, both of us only just 2 years older than the eldest.

Teachers and Learners

To be in Nepal was every day a learning experience for Naomi and me. We got on well. She was intending to study dentistry on her return to Wales but was determined to experience anything and everything that was going. It is not false modesty to acknowledge that as western girls go, she was much more obviously attractive to young men than me, not least to the 16-year-olds we taught but she was also more than capable of observing proper boundaries and could take good care of herself in any situation.

She was amazed when I told her that I had never had a boyfriend and no sexual experience, whereas her accounts of life in Bala at first shocked, but then highly amused me, as she recounted stories of what young people in the Welsh-speaking towns and villages found to occupy their time with. It was hard to decide whether I envied her or not. I had to rethink the meaning of the Welsh song: "We'll keep a welcome in the hillsides"!

Laughter was very much the order of our first days in school, but the process of inculturation, seeking to get inside the mental processes of those living in a very different world from that from which I had come which increasingly occupied my thoughts when not working. How different were their ways of thinking from our own and how could I learn from them? To be honest our work was not exhausting and needed only perfunctory preparation with the younger children; a little more was necessary for the older who had already acquired the rudiments of English, even if mostly through their exposure to American television. For relaxation I went walking in the foothills of the Himalayas, which sounds much grander than it was, but the backdrop to the lives of everyone here was breathtaking and must have influenced their worldview.

The predominant religion of Nepal is Buddhist, though one of the first things I had to learn about it is that as with Christianity, it is made up of many different sorts and traditions, called Schools. What I encountered in Nepal as Buddhism bears very little resemblance to that practised in Japan, Thailand or Sri Lanka. I suppose I had always assumed Buddhists all practised meditation, but I found no indication of this in any of the homes we were invited to visit. There were many religious trinkets in most houses and across the town a huge number of flags with prayers imprinted being released to bring blessings to the world, but in practice seemed to me to amount more to superstition than anything I had anticipated from my few encounters with Buddhism in the West. It often centred on what I came to think of as the cult of the dead, built around forebears and antecedents, honouring them as in some way still present in the many pictures of their departed loved ones in each house.

I also was surprised to find how influential Hinduism was, as I had always thought of it as belonging to India. Kathmandu had contained a number of Hindu Temples, and I came to understand that in practice in local communities there was a considerable amount of syncretism with Buddhists and Hindus both more than willing to share each other's feasts and celebrations.

I can imagine that someone from Nepal coming to the West would find it hard to make sense of American-style evangelicalism, Russian Orthodoxy and High Mass in a Catholic Cathedral all meant to be the same religion, though come to think of it, I found that difficult too.

The mystery of the husband of Hanka was sorted by the sharp eyes of Naomi. She had noticed a photograph of a young man in uniform and looking at it had by now learned the Nepalese for "dad" which Hanka's son proudly pointed out. He was a Gurkha, in Nepalese *Gorkhali*, and was based in the UK whilst we were in Hilepani. We discovered it was a great honour to be selected after rigorous training to serve in the Brigade within the British Army, and it was clear that Hanka relied heavily on the wages her husband earned wherever he was serving. The Brigade of Gurkhas, exclusively recruited from Nepal, has a wonderful history of service, and generally regarded as the toughest and most feared of all British soldiers with their famed and scary kukri knives. It did, however, separate families from their soldiers for long periods, not least because already receiving lower pay than British soldiers and sending much of their money home, they could not easily afford the flight and transport home.

In parallel with schools in the UK, ours had a mid-term break, which Project Trust encouraged us to use to travel and explore the country. Naomi and I felt secure enough to do different things and although we enjoyed one another's company, a break would do us good. She wanted to go further north, up towards the Himalayas to be nearer Everest and so joined one of the buses of what I might describe as the "hippy trail" to Phaphlu where she might even be able to obtain a flight up near the mountain itself.

I was sufficiently intrigued by my contacts with Buddhism to want to visit a monastery and see if there was more to the practice than superstition and the cults of the dead. There was a car hire company in Janakpur but Hanka warned me against it as she thought they might take advantage of a young woman travelling alone, and in any case it would mean a long bus journey out of my way to attempt what might prove less than what I was seeking, so instead of four days away it was back to the bus, with hairpins and drops to the rivers below.

I was on my way to Namobuddha Monastery one of many serving Tibetan refugees and hordes of visitors who regard it as incredibly photogenic, and of course that is what I found on first experience of golden-topped temples and beautiful buildings built on to the hillside. Later, one such building was to be my home for several years, but in Scotland.

The immediate appeal was inevitably aesthetic though I found myself hesitant about taking photographs and there is no way I could possibly do so in the Temple. As those who have visited such a Temple will know, as soon as you enter you are almost immediately overwhelmed by gold and red. There were literally hundreds of golden Buddha statues filling every space of the wall, together with a few *thangkas*, huge Tibetan wall paintings showing in glorious colour things I simply knew nothing about. There were also seating places along sides of the Temple cordoned off, presumably for the members of the community, and what could only be described as a throne in the centre, alongside of which was a small gong. To my initial amusement there was also an electric prayer wheel, also in gold, with words etched on it, as with the flags I had often seen, sending out prayers for the world. In terms of huge understatements, it was different to my occasional encounters with the Church of Scotland back in North Berwick!

I was booked in for two nights and as I made my way to my dormitory, I occasionally saw figures in long red robes and shaven heads, all looking, to me, like the photograph I had seen of the Dalai Lama. Something inside me, however, was saying that this was a special place, not just a tourist attraction.

Exhausted by the journey and shock of the new, I went straight to sleep but had set my watch for 4:30am. I had seen a notice which spoke of something called Tara Prayers in the Temple at 5:00 followed by a meditation session, and I was determined to attend. I took off my shoes and entered the Temple not having the first idea of what I should do, but there were a couple of young people there before me who directed me to a chair against the back wall of the Temple and I sat there, looking around me and wondering.

The community (which I later learned to call the *Sangha*) came in and took their places separately and, like the two young people in front of me, adopted a position of what seemed to me a quite impossible use of legs but no one seemed to be in agony.

No one who has ever heard Tibetan prayers is likely to forget the experience, nor necessarily want to repeat it! Deep voices chant, often for a quite a long time and I had no idea what the words were. But I was entranced. Deep certainly spoke to my shallow in a way that made me want to know more. After Tara Prayers which lasted almost 30 minutes, one of the monks moved and ascended the throne, crossing his legs as before, and after settling rang the gong. There now followed about two more minutes of chanting before I entered my first experience of silent meditation.

But obviously, I had no idea what I should be doing. What was I supposed to meditate about and how did it differ from just thinking? And yet, even in my total inner confusion I felt I was doing something that came naturally. All those hours sitting staring at the sea were almost an ideal preparation. When after an hour, during which I heard nothing suggesting movement among the Sangha, the monk on the throne rang the gong, gave a broad smile and everyone stood and began to make their way out. I had not been crossed-legged, but my bum really hurt when I stood, which I thought really funny and gave a big smile.

'You seem happy,' said one of the young men in English who had shown me in.

'Have read you "The Lord of the Rings"?' I asked him.

'Yes.'

'I think it was when Sam Gamgee had reached Rivendell he said to Frodo, that being there was like being on holiday and at home at the same time.'

He nodded.

'But didn't he go on to say that they still had work to be accomplished?'

'Well, thanks for spoiling that,' I said with a laugh.

'How long are you here?'

'Just one more night and then I return to my work as a teacher in a village 80 miles away called Hilepani.'

'May I say that although you were behind me during prayers and meditation, I was aware of your presence by the quality of your silence.'

'You couldn't hear what was passing inside my head though.'

He laughed.

'Then it a wondrous gift as a first step to notice that. Would you welcome a conversation over some breakfast porridge?'

'Thank you. Yes, I would like that.'

As we walked towards the dining area, he turned to me.

'My name is Brett, by the way.'

'I'm Lizzie and I'm from Scotland. But are you Nepalese, because if so, your English is outstanding?'

He laughed.

'My mother is Nepalese, but my dad is an Australian and that's where I grew up, so technically neither of us speak real English.'

I laughed.

'But what's a Scot doing here travelling alone?' Brett continued. Most of those who come here are either tourists or pilgrims. I'm not completely sure which category you fit?'

'That's encouraging,' I replied. 'I'm not sure I fit any category. But I'm here in Nepal for a year teaching English at two schools in Hilepani, and it's the mid-term break. I've been intrigued by the small amount of Buddhism I've seen in the town to want to find out if there's more to it, and this monastery is probably the nearest where a woman can stay. But I'm not a tourist.'

'No. I can tell that.'

'But which are you?'

'I came here to learn the dharma, Buddhist life and practice. My mother came from a small village near here and it seemed the obvious place to come to learn more. It's not one of the more important monasteries even though the tourists still call in with their cameras and we don't seem to get a lot of pilgrims mainly because we're not all that commercialised, but I like it here.'

We were now seated with our porridge bowls before us.

'How long have been here?'

'Two years in December.'

'Gosh, and are you finding what you came for?'

'Definitely not, because I was coming for what I thought I knew in advance, and what I have begun to discover is completely different. Buddhism, as practised by millions of people, is not the same as seeking to live the dharma. I have stayed because I need to learn much more.'

'When you speak of learning, do you mean acquiring information, the sort of things one might do in a university, reading and studying texts and the like?'

'There is certainly much to learn about, but the simplest of monks who can barely read and certainly not engage in ancient philosophy, knows much more. That is why you and I have spent time together in silence for an hour already and there will be more opportunities for that later in the day and into the night. And, if you will allow me to say, it is why I am intrigued by you.'

'Me?'

'Yes. I told you earlier that I was at once struck by the quality of your silence. Most of the time as humans we are struck by the noises people make, a good singer say, or someone with a gruff voice, but here I have been attuning myself to hearing what isn't spoken, what I call a silent song.'

'Shouldn't your mind have been somewhere else other than on me?' I said with a slight giggle. 'Besides which, by the end, my silence was nearly interrupted by the pain in my bum.'

'I understand that, believe you me. Sitting for an hour and a half first in semi and then in full lotus position is an introduction to pain of a wholly unexpected kind especially when you then attempt to stand and fall over. But, please, Lizzie, it was not a chat-up line, I meant what I said.'

'And if I wanted to learn about what you call the dharma, and I only learned the term a few minutes ago, what do I do next?'

'You have already begun, and the practice of silent meditation is what you continue. Don't read books and acquire knowledge. Just do it.'

'How long are you staying here, Brett?'

'I have no idea. I didn't think I'd be here this long, and I have no plans to leave.'

'Would you be thinking of becoming a monk?'

'There would be only one reason for doing that – only if thereby the practice of dharma was enhanced and strengthened. And I have a long way to go, as proved by my attentiveness this morning during meditation to a lovely Scottish woman!'

'I shall blush in a moment.'

He laughed.

'Please forgive me. That was not my intention. I am what is called a beginner.'

'After two years?'

'It would take many years to learn the art of climbing before I would dare to tackle Kanchenjunga, so it is with the dharma.'

'Not Everest?'

'The queues are too long! There will be a cable car installed soon and a MacDonalds at the top. But now, Lizzie, I must go to my appointed work. Perhaps we shall see one another again in the morning. I hope so.'

Brett rose from his seat, and I remained trying to take in what I had just been given as my first ever instruction in the dharma, which seemed to amount to being told to do nothing other than just to be.

Christmas at Hilepani

Arriving back in Hilepani with an enormous amount to think about (or was it, *not* to think about?), I gathered that Naomi had enjoyed her trip north. Yes, the sight of Everest was wonderful, but even more for her was the chance to meet other young people from Europe and the US, and to have a whale of a time in the evenings! I decided to wait to hear rather than probe, but most of her conversations were about an American student called Hilary, for whom she had clearly fallen in a big way. At first, I assumed Hilary was a man, and then stunned when it turned out she was not a man. Furthermore, Naomi said Hilary was coming to Hilepani in two days' time to see her, and could I cover her teaching for the time Hilary was here.

I grew up in North Berwick and although I regularly went into Edinburgh and watched some television, I had never knowingly spoken to someone who was gay, male or female. My school produced big rugby players. So, I was in unfamiliar territory and found myself wondering (or was it worrying) what this meant sharing a room with a gay woman. I decided to say nothing, because I knew nothing, and happily took on Naomi's work whilst Hilary came to stay.

When she came, I couldn't see what possibly Naomi could find attractive about her. She was loud, had very short hair and more tattoos than in the annual Edinburgh Festival events at the Castle, but much too direct for me about her sexuality. I thought her a tourist rather than a pilgrim, and I feared at once that Naomi was one of the sights, from which she would move on to the next, and what would be left behind other than the sort of junk that already was said to clutter Base Camp of Everest, except that this junk might well be a young Welsh girl.

'You didn't like Hilary, did you?' Naomi said after her departure.

'Naomi, you are my friend and I care for you. I feared that your loneliness, which if we are honest is something we both feel at times, led you to accept the role Hilary wanted of you.'

'But I did so knowingly, Lizzie. You fear Hilary was using me, but perhaps I was using her much more than she can possibly have known. I wanted the sex, and she was good at it. It was no more than that.'

'Oh.'

'Hey, please don't think I shall sneak across the room into your bed one of the nights.'

'Should I take that as a compliment or insult?' I said, laughing.

'I hope I would never hurt anyone by taking advantage of them and I knew Hilary was immune to that. You, Lizzie are my best, and come to think of it, my only friend. But I think it's time for you to tell me about your days away, because I can tell something happened, though I've no idea what.'

'Yeah, well that makes two of us, but something happened, even though it was also nothing at all.'

'That doesn't make sense.'

'I know, but for now, honestly it's the best I can do.'

From the time when I returned to Hilepani through to the day on which I am writing this, many years later, sitting doing nothing has been a permanent feature of my life.

By November, both Naomi and I could make ourselves understood and could understand at least some Nepalese even though I could never quite get to terms with its written forms. I was enjoying teaching and being with children who wanted to learn, absorbing new thoughts and ideas as easily as the air which at that altitude was undoubtedly purer than in the UK.

Ahead of us lay a month-long holiday over what would be regarded in Scotland as the Christmas and Hogmanay holiday, and which Project Trust hoped we might use to travel and explore the country in which we had been placed. Naomi told me that her parents were paying for her to fly back to Wales for a couple of weeks which I was disappointed by, and feared she might not have returned (all that naughtiness in Bala proving too much of a counter attraction!) and I set about wondering what I would do. Then came a phone call from mum and dad saying they wanted to come and visit me here which thrilled me enormously. So, Naomi and I set off by bus back to Kathmandu airport, my mum and dad arriving on the flight that would return Naomi to Manchester, early next morning

I was so excited to see them, and they were somewhat astonished to find it was not as cold as they had expected nor was there any snow. We spent a night in a hotel near the airport before seeing Naomi off on the following day and then spent a few days in the city itself – my first visit too. My initial reaction was one of disappointment as it seemed the place existed only for the benefit of tourists and was extremely garish. The temples disappointed me too as there seemed so little of what I had known at Namobuddha Monastery, everything given over to what could be sold to the idiots who came from afar and knew no better. On the other hand, some western food made a nice change, but it was the company of mum and dad that I most enjoyed.

'Tomorrow,' I said, 'it's the great bus ride. Don't expect comfort or speed, and when we're passing a ravine don't look down.'

Mum looked horrified and then laughed, hoping I was joking.

On the next day they discovered that this was no joke, but they loved the countryside and the sight of the mountains where there was real snow.

'We're protected here from the worst of the winter weather by the mountains. Before I came, I expected deep snows and freezing cold, and though it can be cold at night, local woollen clothing works wonders.'

Hanka and her children received mum and dad with characteristic warmth and dhal. She also offered me the use of the jeep to take them around though I was hesitant having barely driven since getting here and only having passed my driving test just two months before I came. I said that it would be much safer for mum and dad for us to use the buses, though I'm not sure mum would have agreed had she known what I was saying in my basic Nepalese, having spent most of the journey from Kathmandu with her eyes tight shut!

At this stage I felt unable to say anything to mum and dad about my stay at the monastery nor the practice of silent sitting I was engaging in for two period of 30 minutes each day – but not with crossed legs! Nor did I mention that after leaving them at the airport at the end of their stay I was intending to spend another four nights there.

After a Christmas meal of curry, mum and dad produced small gifts for each of the children, one of which was a toy soldier in a kilt. This excited them because it reminded them of their own father in England and that Gurkhas also sometimes wear kilts as part of their dress uniform. For Hanka, they brought a tam-o'-shanter which she continued to wear for the whole of my remaining stay (probably also in bed, and perhaps still to this day!). For me they brought a hardback edition of The Oxford Book of English Verse, which I used extensively in my four years at Uni. I gave them each a *Khata*, the white scarf common in Tibetan Buddhism, as a sign of welcome, honour and respect. They were clearly very moved to receive them. My mum and I cried at the airport, and I knew I would miss them, but I also was still wondering if within a few days Naomi would be landing and returning to Hilepani.

As I made my way by an extremely circuitous route to Namobuddha Monastery, I found myself wondering why I was doing so. It was by any standards an odd thing for an 18-year-old girl to be doing, travelling alone (though in passing I have to say that I never once felt at any kind of risk as I did so). Was I wanting to return simply so I could meet up with Brett again, or was it something else drawing me?

In the deep mid-winter, I had the guest centre almost to myself. It was so good to see Brett again and I recognised other monastic faces that gave me smiles as they passed me engaged in their many chores. Brett told me he had asked the Sangha, the gathered community, to accept him as what in the west we would call a novice monk, here a *samanera*. It didn't assume an intention to make an eventual life commitment, as some young people spent time in a monastery almost as they might in a university back home, but it would bind Brett to the sangha for his testing of the life, and their testing of him. He also had a new name, *Jampa*, a name meaning "gentle voice".

However, his new status meant he was no longer allowed to associate with visitors, and the monk overseeing pilgrims, whilst friendly, had little or no English. That meant I was given even more time alone and in silence. With mum and dad just having departed for Scotland, I won't deny I shed some tears and felt very alone, but it did prepare me, though I didn't know this at the time, for far longer isolations to come.

On my final morning, having packed my rucksack, I was sitting on the steps of the Temple before going out to the road to wait for the bus, when someone in a saffron robe came and sat next to me. It was Brett, now Jampa.

'I knew you would return,' he said, 'and I know too that there will be another day, perhaps many days, weeks, months and years ahead, when you will return. I look forward to that day.'

I stared at him, and he gave me a wide smile, before standing and continuing the work for which he had been appointed. I could not reply and perhaps no reply was possible.

My sole concern on going back to Hilepani after the winter break was whether Naomi would return. In many ways her sense of being cut off from her home and all that that involved in terms of close friendships was greater than my own, and I could well have understood had she not returned. So it was with a real sense of joy when I saw her emerging from the bus. We hugged and kissed.

'I was scared that you wouldn't want to come back once you'd tasted again the flesh-pots of North Wales.'

'I did have a better Christmas dinner than you probably did, even in Kathmandu, but most of my time was spent in my comfortable bed missing you, so of course I came back. And I'm so glad you're back,' she added, 'I didn't know whether you might have turned into a Buddhist nun.'

The children's welcome as school began again was such a joy. I realised just how much I had missed them in the weeks since the end of term, and they all seemed keen to get going with their English classes. And best of all was the welcome from Hanka and her three children who had missed Naomi and me so very much. For us she was cooking a special meal, she told us, though other than the addition of lamb to the curry, it was what we were used to every day!

As we sat in our room that evening, we each tried to say something of how the winter holiday had been spent. I spoke of my days with mum and dad in Kathmandu and, to my surprise, of my slight disappointment that I had not been able to spend more time with Brett, now Jampa.

'Were you hoping for something?' she asked.

'I imagine in a sort of silly "18-year-old who's never had a boyfriend sort of way" I might have been, but he has a destiny to seek, and I could only want to wish him the very best. We did sneak a few moments together before I caught the bus and it struck me how selfless he was being in choosing this life, in which the negating of the self seems to lie at its heart.'

'You do know that you're quite a scary person, don't you?'

'What do you mean by that?' I said, startled.

'I sometimes think you're the deepest person I've ever known, so self-contained and intelligent. I feel quite inadequate alongside you. If you can excuse my language, the infamous Hilary who came here, was terrified of you and the questions you asked her which made her certain you would find out what a fraud she was!'

'She wasn't a fraud, Naomi. She also was looking for something and simply had no idea where or what that might be. If you recall, I was concerned she was making use of you, and perhaps she thought she was, but I laughed and laughed within when you told me it was you making use of her! I was so pleased.'

'Then you should say these things, share the shallow end of the swimming pool with the thicko Welsh girl sometimes. Nobody can live so intensely all the time as you, Lizzie. I know you like your times of silence, but you also need to balance them with noise and the sheer enjoyment of your extreme good fortune of being here with me.'

I gave her a huge hug, and our tears flowed.

If Brett was my first Buddhist teacher, then without a shadow of a doubt my second was Naomi, even if she would never have seen herself in that role, but she taught me something so very special, though it would take many years for me to learn it, and it would be my closest friend, whom I was to call my sister, who told me that she had been told by the person who had most inspired her own life that in essence whatever else we might mean by the spiritual life, it was always about total normality. She hadn't known that he was in fact quoting a 9th century Chinese Buddhist called *Linji Yixuan*:

"Just act ordinarily, without trying to do anything in particular. Move your bowels, piss, get dressed, eat your rice, and if you get tired, lie down".

In later years, I was to hear a story from the 4th century Egyptian desert which echoes this. The founder of Christian monasticism, Anthony of Egypt, was once asked why he allowed his monastics to have times of relaxation. He replied by asking the man to string his bow and fire an arrow, and then another and then another until the man protested that doing so would damage the bow. Anthony of Egypt had made his point that doing the same to his monks would damage them too!

Basant Ritu, or Springtime, is both the best and worst time in Nepal. The climate is delightful and the foliage so beautiful, and the people begin to come alive too as they do the world over when winter fades. But it is also the time when the hordes of trekkers and tourists come, many of them passing through, changing buses to head towards Everest. It brought a measure of income to the street traders, and I smiled at the way tourists bought the Buddhist trinkets, beads, prayer flags, singing bowls and more, to take home to give as presents, perhaps imagining that they had captured something of Buddhism.

It was now quite possible for us to teach the children in the open air which we did as much as possible. There was a moment that each of us separately experienced the question of just what it was we were teaching, when one young man said to me, "Och Lizzie...", and a girl said to Naomi in an almost perfect Welsh accent, "How green the valley is", pointing to the area near the school! We reported this to the person appointed by Project Trust who came to pay us a visit and see how we were managing so far away from home and both of us still only 18. She thought this hilarious but was able to report back to Coll that all was well and that we were intending to use the last weeks of our stay to do some trekking together across the Border into the far north of India, to visit Darjeeling and head north into the Khangchendzonga National Park, where I could visit the 3rd largest mountain in the world and widely regarded by Buddhists and Hindus alike as the most holy, Kanchenjunga.

It was the most awesome sight, far more so than Everest and although there were still many visitors to the area, by rising at 4:00 I was able for three days to go out and sit in contemplation of this astonishing peak. I could begin to understand how it might be that Tibetan Buddhism, formed against the backcloth of these mountains, containing in themselves both beauty and extreme danger, had taken the form it has.

The coming of summer meant that most of our children were out of school, working in the fields and we had little to do other than simply enjoy being part of Hanka's family and the community of Hilepani. My Nepalese was by now good, and I knew how much the people of the town had warmed to Naomi and me. Often in the evening, in what is their harvest time, we enjoyed wonderful Nepalese parties with the children around us making sure I didn't imbibe too much of the local version of Rakshi, made from millet and brewed in clay pots. It had a kick like a mule as I discovered the very first time I tried it (and spent two days recovering!). I suspect Naomi had been more used to alcohol and survived without too much difficulty, but it did not stop her mocking the "poor wee Scots lassie who canna hold her drink".

As the time of our departure drew near, I did wonder whether I might make a final pilgrimage to Namobuddha Monastery, but reflected that at this time of the year it would be almost wholly awash with tourists and their wretched cameras, and that, in any case, it would be highly unlikely that I would get to see the former Brett, now *Jampa*, the gentle voice. I did still endeavour (Rakshi notwithstanding) to spend time in silence each day and felt it was one of the greatest gifts Nepal had given to me as I returned to North Berwick and the prospect of 4 years study of English literature.

Literature and the City

It has long been a tradition in Scotland that students attend the university nearest to their home, not least to save money by not having to pay for halls of residence. There were of course some who chose English universities, but we were proud of the great traditions of the Scottish universities, Edinburgh, Glasgow, Aberdeen and St Andrews as being at least on a par and often better than any in England.

I had little time once I was home to prepare for the new life in a big city and with people whose fervent activity clashed so markedly with my experience of the past year. I elected to live in a hall of Residence, but mostly it was with first-year girls straight from school, younger than myself whose catchphrase seemed to be "the wilder the better". The Hall was often extremely noisy and increasingly I returned to North Berwick allowing me time to be quiet, to reflect on the lessons of the past year in Nepal and above all to throw myself into the sheer delight of four years reading for sheer enjoyment.

I loved discovering the parts of the city I didn't know, though I already knew that it had to be avoided completely from mid-July through to the end of August when the world-famous Festival was being held and the city flooded with people from everywhere other than Scotland!

In terms of my academic discoveries, I focussed increasingly on poetry and especially that of Auden, Eliot, but above all on the works of the 17th century English poets sometimes labelled the "metaphysicals": George Herbert, John Donne, Henry Vaughan and the unusual writings of their near contemporary Thomas Traherne. If for one moment I could have imagined that present-day Christianity in any way reflected or gave expression to these profound traditions I might have wondered if my own spiritual journey could have found a home there, but I knew it was not so. All the Christian church groups in and out of the university seemed to embody the damning phrase of EM Forster, "Poor little talkative Christianity" and it seemed to me so very often that it spoke of nothing that mattered to someone who had experienced something so very different.

There were several different Buddhist groups in the university, but little echoed the Buddhism I had come to know. Somehow or other, and I cannot exactly recall how, I learned about a Tibetan Buddhist community in Edinburgh called Kagyu Samye Dzong which I began to visit and at once felt at home.

It was related to a Tibetan Buddhist monastery and temple which I was stunned to learn could be found somewhere in the Borders, which had apparently been functioning since 1967 and founded by Tibetan exiles, and hearing about it, I was eager to pay a visit. But I in my third year I had a new major distraction in my life. He was called David and came from Inverbervie, a small village on the same North Sea coast I knew so well, and we found ourselves paired together for tutorials on 19th century literature, which excited neither of us but drew us together in our shared dislike of Jane Austen, Dickens and Trollope. We began to spend more time together and often attended concerts in the many venues offered by the city.

I had still not had a boyfriend until David came on the scene and I was certainly hesitant and probably very slow in taking the relationship on. David was extremely patient with my sexual inexperience though I know he wanted to take things further and establish something that would last. I liked him very much and we regularly went for long walks along the coast which we both loved.

It was a year into our friendship that David decided he had to take the initiative and suggested that as we were both wanting to do a further year teacher training after graduation, we should so living together. By then I knew I had either to accept the suggestion or end the relationship, and I was by now deeply aware that I was beginning to want David close, so I agreed. We found a flat in Musselburgh and with a life of teaching and, presumably, all that went with marriage, I settled down to what stretched before me.

Having graduated with a First and Distinction, my tutors and others were dismayed when I announced that I wanted to be a Primary School teacher. David could not understand this either and trained as a secondary school teacher, so we did not spend a great deal of time together in college, or even out of the learning environment. He was a great sportsman and played soccer for the University teams, including the First XI and had one or two scouts from the big teams expressing interest. I was spending more time at Kagyu Samye Dzong, getting to know members of the small Sangha and sharing periods of meditation with them.

David and I lived together for four years and for almost the whole time we did so quite happily though increasingly we were both attending more to different needs when not working. We enjoyed holidays abroad and my parents enjoyed David's company, as I did his parents. I guess it is to damn with faint praise when I say that I was very fond of David, but to go beyond that, to say that I loved him in the way that he wished, which came in the form of hints and suggestions that we get married, increasingly I knew I could not do so.

My own direction had been increasingly towards regular

contacts and stays at Samye Ling, the Tibetan Monastery 30 or so miles south of Edinburgh. From the day of my first arrival, it very much felt like I was coming home as it reminded me so much of my experience of the Monastery in Nepal. I cannot honestly recall that from my first visit, over a weekend, I felt some sort of calling to become a Buddhist nun, but I have no doubts that something was going on beneath the surface which undoubtedly drew me further and further away from the prospect of permanence with David.

I made the decision to become a fully-fledged Buddhist, the process called "Taking Refuge", which is the statement of intent to live under the shadow of the Buddha's wing, to confirm my life in accordance with Buddha's teaching, notably such as the Four Noble Truths, the Eightfold Path, and the Stages of the Path to Enlightenment. It was not a difficult step because in my reading and practice I had been seeking to live these things for some time. Throughout the year at Samye Ling there are opportunities for men and women take part in the Refuge Ceremony and on the day there were six others, two men and four women with me.

The ceremony is simple but involves a solemn vow made in Tibetan which concludes with the commitment to the Buddha's teaching: "From now until the end of this life, I hold this master to be my spiritual friend." I loved the last two words – spiritual friend – for how wonderful to think of the Buddha not as some sort of Almighty Lord to be feared, but as an intimate whose words are there for our well-being here and now.

Not that I thought everything in the Buddhist, or even the Samye Ling Buddhist, form of religion was perfect. For example, although lip service was paid to the equality of the sexes, in practice this was not so even within the monastic life, nor did I necessarily immediately take to some of those who were regarded highly within the community. Tibetan Buddhist exiles have not always done well in the West faced with the opportunities and temptations it provides, and there are ghastly stories of sexual and alcoholic abuse even within the Sangha, albeit mostly in the United States. And although Samye Ling is what I regard as mainstream Tibetan Buddhism, closely allied to the Dalai Lama who has visited, Buddhism itself in the West is as diverse and oppositional to other strands, almost to the degree of hate, as many Christian traditions are. It was the poet and artist William Blake in his work *Everlasting Gospel* who wrote "The Vision of Christ that thou dost see / Is my Vision's Greatest Enemy", and sadly this is as true in Buddhism as it is in other religious traditions. So, it was not with total blindness to the weaknesses and failures that were increasingly apparent within western Buddhism that I made the commitment to "take refuge" and in the course of the ceremony received a new name, Bahuputtikā Soṇā, meaning one who had many children, but was known in older age as the most dedicated of all female followers of the Buddha. I wasn't immediately convinced this was the most appropriate name, but I endeavoured to welcome it and hoping it did not portend years of birth-giving!

David came to Samye Ling for the ceremony in what was to be his only visit, as did my mum and dad. He found the place culturally impossible and said very little as we all ate together afterwards. Mum and dad, who had come out to Nepal, seemed much more at ease. But they knew, as I did, and I think David did, that our relationship was in decline.

This came to a head whilst we were visiting Paris over the school Easter holiday when he made an ultimatum that we should get married or breakup. Enough to say that we returned separately from this holiday and by the time I returned to our house in Musselburgh he had left.

Of course, I cried and felt very sad because we had been through a lot together, and no doubt some people would think my hesitations were ridiculous, and certainly my mum and dad thought so as they were more than happy to accept David as their son-in-law, but I had no doubt that I was right not to commit myself to something that I had such doubts and hesitations about. Many years on I still have occasional contact with David and rejoice in the fact that he is happily married with two children.

So eventually, having lived alone again for two further years after my parting from David, I took the momentous step of deciding to come to live at Samye Ling, possibly with a view to becoming a nun.

Nun and Solitary

I had to spend a whole year just living and working with the other members of the community. Women were segregated into their own building called *Purelands*, which was often simply wishful thinking when I heard some of the conversations taking place between young female visitors! For the rest of the time however we worked together with the men, increasingly attending to the many visitors, cooking and cleaning but above all receiving teachings and the daily opportunities for extended meditation practice, which for me was the centre of my life there. In the earliest days of my time in Purelands, the heating was unreliable at best and in winter it could be very cold indeed, ironically mostly colder than I had ever experienced in Nepal.

Throughout the previous 10 years since we had been in Nepal together, I had remained in close contact with Naomi and she, together with her now long-term partner, Andrea, a fellow dentist, came to stay at the monastery. This was for both of us a very merry time and I was able to learn that in the previous year she and Andrea had visited Hilepani as they joined the hordes of visitors to gape upon Everest. It was so good to hear news of those who had been children and were now fathers and mothers themselves, and above all to hear that Hanka and her husband, now retired from the Gurkhas, were reunited and living happily together, though I was also saddened to hear of the deaths of two of those I had taught as children.

I'm pleased to say Naomi remained sceptical about my lifestyle here and I've long held onto that distrust because I think that in any major life commitment the capacity for recognising ambivalence is so very important, but it was after their visit that I went to see our retreat master to say that I would wish to explore the possibility of becoming a nun.

Rinpoche, meaning "Precious One", a title given to a special and gifted teacher, which he is, is full of laughter always, but never mocking laughter. He laughs with you and always gently. In that sense he never takes himself so totally seriously that he cannot even see the funny side of himself. But with this outward attractiveness goes an utter dedication to the Buddhist traditions of meditation and he completed what is known as the 49-day *Bardo*, spending the whole period in absolute silence in total darkness. He did this on Holy Island, the tiny Island just off the Isle of Arran.

The vows of a Buddhist nun (or monk) within the Tibetan tradition are taken for life, therefore it is important to spend time and take great care before making a decision. And although there are cases of people who take vows and later give them back and return to lay life, this is not recommended. The vows are taken with the determination to keep them for the rest of one's life.

Becoming a Buddhist monastic means that you are joining a community – the *Sangha*. The purpose of the community is to study and practice the Buddha's teachings, and whenever possible, to share them with others and by tradition one stays in a monastic community for at least 5 years after becoming ordained.

Living in community also means that we share our resources, our habits, our practice and our personalities. In learning to live in a community one can face many difficulties, particularly as many of us have been raised in cultures of individual self-expression, characterised best in the idea of the "selfie" which was beginning to sweep the world. To protect our ordination, the *vinaya* (code of conduct) for monastic life is very explicit in how we live in community.

The process of preparation lasted a further year even though in practice the life I lived as, what in the west monastic traditions would be called, a novice, was not so dissimilar from what I had been doing since arriving to live there. Inevitably in the west, Buddhism is regarded as one religion amongst others, but to Buddhists it is seen as an art rather than a religion, something grown into rather than acquired in one fell swoop. You are always *becoming* a Buddhist, whereas it seems to me you are either a Christian, a Moslem or a Jew, or you are not. To Buddhists this seems an odd way of being and Rinpoche stressed again and again that we would go through the ordination ceremony but becoming a nun would take very much longer.

By now I was familiar with the Tibetan language we used for chanting and although to western ears it can sound almost dirge-like, I think it almost akin to the psalm-singing of the members of the Wee Frees in Scotland and have never ceased to be moved by it. I was also beginning read some Tibetan Buddhist teaching books, many of which had been smuggled out of Tibet over the mountains from China into Nepal.

In the last retreat I made before ordination, I sent a message to Namobuddha Monastery to let Jampa know what I was doing. To my amazement, on the eve of the ordination ceremony I received a reply from him expressing his delight and sending blessings across the thousands of miles between us.

In ordination, we bind ourselves to what are known as the Three Jewels: Buddha, Dharma (the teachings) and Sangha (the community) and we were reminded that in ordination we had to represent those things to all who would look upon us, and judge what we professed by the ways we lived our commitment. It was an awesome thought, and I approached the day without hesitation. I knew that it was for this that I had been born, and that it was not an end but simply a new beginning.

The new clothes received in ordination mark us out as Buddhist monks and nuns and are signs of renunciation, as also is the shorn head and I had to learn how to shave my own head at least once a month. I admit the shock to my vanity when I looked in the mirror once it was done for me the first time by one of the senior nuns, and I wondered what my mum and the others from the family who came to witness my break with the world into which they had brought me and nourished me, would think of it, but if they found it distasteful they didn't say. In winter of course it meant an ever-present woollen hat!

And then on the day after the ordination ceremony, it was back to work as normal, cleaning floors, preparing food, chatting to visitors at mealtimes but above all continuing to live out the precepts I had now taken for life, centred on meditation and the ethical demands of Buddhism, though they are as much for lay Buddhists as the Sangha.

Some six months or so later, Rinpoche asked me if I could at late notice, stand in for one of the other nuns who was ill and due to help lead one of the many courses we run at Samye Ling. Perhaps my Primary School Teaching skills came to the fore because most of the those who come to stay are either beginners or at an early stage in their growing, and I seem to have hit the right note. It occurred to me afterwards that perhaps the other nun had not been so ill after all, and that Rinpoche was trying me out as a teacher. At mealtimes many of the young women who came would often come and ask me questions, ostensibly about my life, but in reality, about their own lives.

I was happy and settled, but inside I knew I wanted something more and that was how I asked Rinpoche if he would consider me for the long three-year, three-month, three-day retreat on Holy

Isle. I heard nothing from him for two months and assumed he had either forgotten or decided against, and then one morning as I was mopping the kitchen floor he came in and quite simply told me to prepare myself and my family for this next stage of my Buddhist life.

The tiny Holy Isle, (not to be confused with Holy Island or Lindisfarne, off the Northumberland coast) lying to the east of the Isle of Arran, was bought by Samye Ling in 1992, and from the beginning was not just intended as a Buddhist Centre but to create and provide an ecologically sustainable environment where individuals could develop and experience inner peace, regardless of their background or spiritual tradition. However, certain parts of the island are closed to visitors, notably what is known as the Inner Light Retreat at the southern tip of the island where the first Buddhist three-year, three-month, three-day retreat took place and was completed in 2006 by 12 women. There is a further retreat base on Arran for men, who began their first long retreat in 2005.

On the island can be found many Buddhist statues, flags and stupas, small white ornamental structures, the first thing you see when you leave the boat on arrival. I had grown used to seeing them in Nepal and they are symbols of the enlightened mind of Buddha and are intended to restore and balance ourselves, transforming negative energies.

We were each allotted a room, as in Purelands, characterised by simplicity, and it was here that I would spend the next three years and three months and three days in silence and alone, apart from gathering together in the meditation hall for some teaching with no conversation permitted.

To my mum and dad, and no doubt to my dear friend Naomi, the very idea of this commitment, on top of what they might already have decided was a bizarre decision to take monastic vows, this must have seemed utterly bizarre. Before leaving Samye Ling to make the journey to the Island I wrote to them saying that though I could understand they could not understand what I was doing, I was sure this was the right next step for me and urged them to know I would not let a day go by without thinking of them. I could receive letters from a small number of those closest to me but there was no facility available for telephone or any other means of communication.

The schedule of retreat life was demanding, based mainly on meditation practice in four three-hour sessions. The daily wake-up time was 3:00 am with the first main session starting at 4:00 am, prefaced by Tibetan chanting. The various practices and meditations changed each year, in accordance with instruction from Rinpoche, the retreat master. Each day concluded with a series of further chanted Tibetan prayers and I was usually in my bed and asleep by 10:00 pm.

In the course of my time a small number of other retreatants, and an equally small number of men on Arran also living the retreat, decided to leave but this never occurred to me as an option. I did however have access to writings not just about aspects of the Tibetan spiritual tradition, but also to books about others living as solitaries. I especially read a lot about Fr Thomas Merton who had spent the later years of his time as a Cistercian monk living in a hermitage in Kentucky in the United States, who felt that the solitary life was what he was made for (even though he entertained large numbers of visitors to the hermitage), but was fascinated by his own move towards Buddhism, not least on his final visit to Nepal where he met the Dalai Lama and other monks and saw for himself mighty Kanchenjunga. Equally I learned about our own Buddhist solitaries, and those in the early desert traditions of the Christian fathers in the 4th and 5th centuries. I knew too that there were solitaries living in the UK today and I was especially interested to learn about the Carthusian monks living as solitaries at St Hugh's Charterhouse in Parkminster, Sussex and that, which was astonishing news to me, there were even a small number of

Anglicans living the solitary life, so if I was a lunatic, then it struck me I was in very good company.

The decision to allow someone to make the long retreat is not easy. The principal requirement is mental stability and a deep-rooted experience of meditation over many years. Without both it would be quite impossible and indeed dangerous. Later I would meet someone who had five years of solitary silence in which she learned the art of meditation almost from zero but backed up by an astonishing mental stability.

Silence

Speaking about silence is in many ways the ultimate oxymoron but I will take the risk because many have asked me about it. Looking back over such questions, the one I have been most often asked is, "What good does it do?" – the implication being that religious activity must result in doing good in the world or else they are just a form of self-indulgence.

Because I believe Buddhism is essentially an art, there is a straightforward parallel with the work of other artists who do things: compose, paint, write, simply because they choose to do them, often because they have inside themselves the drive to create. The solitary is like that. It is no less a response to what he or she discovers within and requires no justification. Having said that, however, I do not know what the effect is on others of my hours in meditation. I was certainly aware in my first two years of the evil in the world. I guess that the desert fathers thought this was the activity of demons, but unless we are totally insensitive to suffering around us, we each of us carry the impact of what we see, whether close to, in our friends and family, or through the medium of television and social media. It is something I experienced in the silence, that drawing of evil into the silence and living with it, perhaps even in some way transforming it. Hopefully what we learn is *Karuṇā*, which although normally translated as "compassion" doesn't just mean being nice, but embodying a commitment to all beings, especially those who suffer. I keep with me words from a lay American Buddhist many years ago in which she talks about the need for courage for compassion:

"The courage of compassion is said to come from equanimity. Because we feel compassion in response to seeing pain we need equanimity to be able to open to the pain. In order to not deny it or pretend it's not there or repackage it so it sounds better or looks better, we need to actually see it for what it is. We need equanimity, we need courage, we need wisdom to be able to open to pain. And then the compassion can come forth."

It was when, some years after my solitude, I saw this courage in action, true compassion, that I made an even bigger change than those of taking refuge, ordination or the silent retreat. But I do not think I could have recognised that *Karuṇā* without having spent so many hours alone in silence.

I won't deny that I found the endless days and months of silence tough at times, and it sometimes required a disciplined mind and body to engage in the long hours of sitting meditation, but oddly I never experienced loneliness, and two years in I began to experience a different quality of silence in that all the junk I carried with me in my brain began to disturb me less. I even felt as if I could understand some of what I had previously thought of as the esoteric teachings I received, not by using any kind of logical thought, but by allowing them to soak into me by a form of spiritual and mental osmosis. I discovered that some things cannot be learned by thinking but only by entering into the very processes that had led my forebears to speak out of that same knowledge.

Sometimes, as I know was the case for Thomas Merton in his hermitage, I would sing songs aloud. I had always loved the work of Simon and Garfunkel and many were the days when I yelled out the words of "Bridge over troubled water" and "The Boxer".

Far from being intrusions these served to enrich the giving of myself to a total renunciation and when I spoke of this to Rinpoche, he encouraged me to sing whatever I wished.

In the winter months it was cold and dark, and I wondered if I could ever survive the 49-day *Bardo* retreat in silence and total darkness that Rinpoche had undertaken here on Holy Isle. Our food was nourishing but unbelievably boring and repetitive, and I do recall at least a couple of days when my poor brain became fixated on the idea of a Big Mac, even though it was many years since I had eaten one, having been vegetarian for over a decade. But this was a classic example of how the brain, or at least the left-side of the brain which likes to organise everything and take charge, and which was undoubtedly expressing intense frustration that there were no plans for it to make, throws up all sorts of distractions to lead us astray. I don't just mean those living my silent sort of life, but all of us who find our minds obsessed with something, whether the trivial idea of a burger or something much more serious and potentially damaging to ourselves and others. Having the vision of that burger before me provided me with an excellent opportunity to see my mind in action, discovering how best to respond to all the things that the stimuli of the world and advertising throw before us. It was the same for the desert monks, offered young naked women in their minds. Their demons, however, were not the product of an external devil, but were there within their own minds. In that sense the years, months and days I spent in silence were an experience of self-discovery and self-awareness, or at least I hoped they were.

Many people have told me that they find meditation difficult and express surprise, and perhaps a little disappointment, when I tell them that it is so because it is demanding. I have sometimes been helped in my understanding of how this is so from the occasional western writer. Merton, yes, but long before him, I learned to appreciate the works of the two-16th century Spanish saints, Teresa of Avila and her close companion John of the Cross. The context in which they write, that of counter-reformation catholic theology, means nothing to me, but as a Buddhist seeking to understand and practice more, I recognise much that they taught. Neither were the sort of plaster-saints Catholics seem to love and which are a huge turn-off to me. They taught and functioned against a background of enormous struggle and difficulties.

Rinpoche knew that I was reading these two Carmelites and gave his approval. It's not that he doesn't recognise boundaries between faiths but the presence of other religious traditions among those who come to the isle shows how he understood that it is an ecumenism shared by those who have lived the very experiences we each had known whatever the context and circumstances. We may not ever be able to share words, but we recognise the song of silence familiar to those who have lived this life. Frustrating though it is to those who cannot hear this song and then pepper us with questions about our apparent uselessness, we need give no answers and mostly cannot do so. How can we explain colour to the blind?

In other religious traditions to my own, spiritual blindness and deafness are likewise challenges to someone taking the risk of entering a very different pattern of life in which suddenly something makes sense that previously confounded our capacities to grasp. There is an analogy of which I learned from my former partner, David. He played the clarinet, and he told me that when you begin to learn what is known as the upper register is quite inaccessible, however hard you try. And then once the basics of the clarinet in the lower register have been acquired, one day suddenly the upper register is there, and you never even knew how.

There is, I later learned, a Greek word μετάνοια (metanoia) which in the Christian scriptures is customarily translated as repentance, being sorry for your sins and resolving to try harder.

But the Greek word is subtler than that, because literally the Greek word means a "change of mind". This is not just a matter of changing the content of our thinking, replacing one set of things with another, however religious in content, but implies a change in the way we do our thinking. That could almost define what we aim for in meditation, not replacing one lot of junk with another.

This where I must give expression to the fundamental difference between meditation and mindfulness which has become so very popular in various forms across the world. I do not want to lose sight of how very useful mindfulness can be to so many people in terms of helping them cope in the world as it has become, so very fast and noisy. But this is not the same as Buddhist meditation. In the first place it is customarily being sold as a tool for self-enhancement, improving our performance in the world, and inevitably, to make us feel better about ourselves. Despite the aggrandisement of the self, which is wholly contrary to Buddhist meditation, Buddhist meditation is considerably more than these things and although some of the techniques offered by so-called teachers are recognisable to Buddhists as drawn from their own practice of meditation, it is only in the very earliest of stages that this is so.

As a teacher of meditation, I always make it clear that in entering into serious Buddhist meditation you are going well beyond just stilling the mind. The only reason for meditation is the wish to enter truth itself. Why else would we wish to do this bizarre solitary practice if the aim of our existence is not to be drawn into the truth? And we have to be drawn, recognising that we are not capable of getting there by our own efforts however demanding they may be, but that our practice is the necessary part of preparing to be drawn.

The day came when we emerged, and we looked at one another and smiled cautiously, and then on Arran at the men also completing their retreat. Once on the mainland a coach took us back to Samye Ling where we were deposited into Purelands. It was a huge shock to be away from our homes on the isle, to be with others and to see the world again in all its busyness, noise and chaos. We didn't immediately seek to speak to one another, making up for all that been spoken for so long, but it did make me realise just how many of the things we say to each other are not exactly necessary, just spoken almost the sake of doing so, because we fear the silence. Homes keep the television on all day as background noise because silence is not golden but terrifying.

It was on a Sunday afternoon that all the returning retreatants were led in procession from Purelands to the Temple for a ceremony followed by meeting up with families and friends in the dining room. I think I speak for all my fellow retreatants that the experience of being reunited with loved ones was considerably more difficult than we might have anticipated, as was reintegration with the Sangha, but over the following months I tried to bring together those amazing years which now I felt had flown by and the day-to-day life of a nun. Rinchope gave me responsibilities especially with women retreatants coming to stay at Purelands, work I very much enjoyed, demanding of me a proper grasp of teachings to give to others, though my constant theme was that of persistence and patience. Meditation is not easy, and I encouraged the (mostly young) women who came to stay for a few days or even longer, never to feel that they had failed when they lost the discipline demanded of practice, whether of meditation itself or the occasional lapse when the thought of a burger arose! More than anything, however, I wanted to speak about *Karuṇā* as the heart and essence of all that Buddha taught.

And then something wholly unexpected happened when I came face to face with a female rabbi at lunch in the dining hall!

Karuṇā

The story of how Elise Westernberg came to Samye Ling has been told in *The Waiting Room*, but it is enough to say that she abandoned the rabbinate and Talmud scholarship to become a solitary living on the North York Moors for five years and living a much more solitary existence than I had known on Holy Isle. There was no teaching, no opportunity to meet with a guide such as Rinpoche and barely any contact with anyone other than a local farmer whom she assisted each morning with his milking, and an occasional visit from a Jewish friend in London.

I had entered a tradition of retreat and absolute withdrawal but for Elise there was nothing comparable. She had been directed to this by a catholic priest living as a hermit in Canada (she is Canadian by birth) who informed her that 30 years earlier when she was just three days old, he had baptised and confirmed her as a Catholic. He told her he had been waiting for her to return and gave her the instruction to go back to the UK and continue his own life work in what he called the Waiting Room, and that is what she did.

She told me that she had gone into the solitary life following too many direct experiences of tragedy and death determined to wait until it was clear how they could be made sense of and integrated into her previous understandings of what Jews call *HaShem* (which simply means The Name, the "G" word being too holy to speak). She took with her too, the reality of knowing her great grandparents had with 6 million other Jews perished in the Holocaust. It was almost a trial of strength which reminded her, she said to me once, of the struggle between Jacob and an angel by a river called Jabbok in the Hebrew Bible. She would wait and not let go.

For her the end of her years in the Waiting Room came when for the second time in her life someone committed suicide whilst talking to her on the telephone. Elise has the most wonderful voice, and I could understand why it might be that someone could find considerable comfort in hearing her speak to them in extremis. On the evening of that day, for the first time in five years she suddenly felt acutely lonely and knew that the time had come to leave the Waiting Room and lay awake wondering what on earth she was supposed do now. She did not have long to wait for on the very next morning whilst helping her local farmer get his cattle tested for TB, Elise and the Dutch vet doing the tests fell hopelessly in love. They married, moved to the Dales and now have three daughters.

Elise came from her five years solitary silence accompanied by what she calls שְׁכִינָה (*Shekinah*), Presence, though she will never say more than that. She is a mum, a wife and a farmer (she used to milk three mornings a week on a local dairy farm three days a week but when the farmer retired, she acquired her own small herd of goats which she milks every day, makes goat cheese and passes the milk on to be sold). Although great care should always be used when applying this sort of language, I think she is the most natural contemplative person I know, and has also continued to attract to herself those facing suffering and death. She eschews almost all religious language but will just about allow herself to speak of a sense of purpose, and no further.

I came late into the dining hall and saw this woman sitting by herself as she too had arrived late. Gathering my food, I asked if I could join her. I cannot recall the content of that first conversation once it had passed the stage of polite introductions, but I knew at once I could almost tangibly feel that this woman was special in a way I could recognise. I invited her for a conversation later in the day and that was when we discovered one another as being almost mirror images. That was perhaps the most astonishing experience of my entire life and to say that I was surprised that I had discovered this in a rabbi, is to say nothing of the explosion in my brain required to make sense of it!

We met again on the following day and shared even more. It was the first time I had felt able to share with anyone, even Rinpoche, the deepest parts of my retreat experience, knowing that they were fully understood by this mother of three who farmed in the Yorkshire Dales, and that all I said was safe with her. For the first time too, she was able to speak "deep-unto-deep" from what she called her "solitary refinement".

She was due to leave on the following day and I was dreading her departure, but that night in the midst of what was to be the worst snowstorm of the winter, I was called by a fellow nun who was also a midwife to attend a dying baby belonging to a young couple who worked at Samye Ling. Although they had both taken refuge, for whatever reasons they wanted their baby baptised before he died. In the middle of the night, and in a blizzard, I knew that getting a minister from Lockerbie to come was out of the question. To me there was only one possibility. I knew that Christian baptism can be performed by any baptised Christian and does not require a priest or minister, and so it was that I summoned Elise from her bed. I told her the situation and without the slightest hesitation said she would baptise the baby. We went out into the night, and I drove her in the Land Rover to the cottage where the couple lived. Elise took over and performed a Christian baptism which she was enabled to do having herself been baptised when just three days old!

As I looked at this incredible act the first word that came to my mind was "miracle", but it was soon replaced by *Karuṇā*, an act of courage and compassion so overwhelming that it was to bring about a major change in my life.

Elise and her two friends, Aishe and Leah, with whom she had come to Samye Ling made their way slowly home through the snow on the following day and I spent much of that day in tears, both of joy that I had been privileged to witness something extraordinary and sorrow that Elise had returned home and I knew that in some way my own future was bound up with her.

We did not communicate in the next few weeks other than in one brief letter I sent telling her about the parents of the baby, but each day I could not remove from my mind what had taken place in that night when an act of courage had brought even a tiny light to new parents whose Christian child had died as we sat with them after the baptism. Three months after the baby died, they decided to move away from Samye Ling and return to Edinburgh, where there is an unusual corollary to this that I shall relate later.

I was unsettled in the days and weeks following that night, though I never spoke of this to anyone, though one or two people had asked if I was ok and of course I replied with a smile and said yes. But I wasn't. Rinpoche had been in America at the time of the baptism, but I'm far from sure I could have spoken to him about it and its effect upon me. I knew that the only person I could now rely on as my spiritual guide was a married woman farmer in Yorkshire who had been ordained as a rabbi some years earlier!

On his return, I went to see Rinpoche and told him I wished to be allowed to leave for a rest period at home with my parents. He denied me permission, but I was not prepared to give up as the sense inside me that I needed to be with Elise grew day by day. Finally, I went to see Rinpoche and said that my future in the

Sangha was at risk if didn't have an opportunity to get right away as soon as possible. Perhaps he feared a breakdown of some sort and so it was that I was given permission to leave, and provided with the means to travel by train and bus to Edinburgh.

I took the very early bus to Lockerbie, travelling in jeans, a sweatshirt and a loose jacket, carrying my robes with me and some food for the journey. Anyone who has ever had to take that bus will know its capacity for inducing travel sickness, swinging round tight beds at speed as it does, but at least none of the other passengers recognised me and I had a woollen hat which concealed my shorn head.

At the railway station the plan I outlined to Rinpoche was to take the train to Glasgow and then change for Edinburgh. Approaching the ticket office, I said, "A single, to Northallerton, please". It was, I suppose a crazy act. I had no real idea how to reach the town where Elise lived with her family but felt that a route that would take me via Carlisle, Newcastle and Northallerton might get me somewhere near. I had not communicated this to Elise, though I had written to my parents saying I had been granted a week's break from the Temple.

I enjoyed the train journeys, especially that across the northernmost railways line in England which eventually began to follow the course of the Tyne, just south of Hadrian's Wall. The posh train out of Newcastle was busy and more comfortable than the two earlier ones had been, but also lacked genuine character. I was on the left-side and so had a wonderful view as the train slowed and entered the station at Durham, the site of the great Cathedral on the hill, said to be the resting place of St. Cuthbert, a Northumbrian hermit who became Bishop of Lindisfarne. I took this to be a good omen. Soon we were on our way again, and once out of Darlington I prepared to leave at the next station stop.

At the bus station in Northallerton a kind official of some sort told me I needed the bus to Hawes (a name which amused me somewhat) outside the Nag's Head. Called the "Wensleydale Flyer", it was driven more sedately than that of the early morning, but as it snaked its way up the dale, I could see ahead the Pennines and the land where I knew Pieter, Elise's husband, made his living caring for animals and farmers alike, often on remote farms. The sheep I began to see in increasing numbers were different from those around us at Samye Ling; not Wensleydales I was to learn, which have become something of a specialist breed, but Swaledales (oddly pronounced *Swardles*) which had rough coats and big horns and seemed to me more than just a handful for a vet to have to manage.

Eventually we reached the town. I had an address but no phone number but assumed that "veterinary surgery" might elicit some sort of information, though the first person I asked turned out to be a visitor from Sweden! There was a wide-open area in the centre of the town, full of cars, and as I was to discover, taken over every Friday by a large market. At the top of this area was the Post Office, and from there I was directed on to the road leading out of the town and at once saw the sign for the veterinary surgery. It struck me that after my journeys in Nepal, today had been quite straightforward. I stood before the door adjacent to the surgery and knocked, in the words of Eliot, "finding the place not a moment too soon". I could not possibly have anticipated what followed.

"It will be Soṇā"

I had removed my woollen hat, and a girl, in her teens, whom I later realised was Grace, opened the door. 'Mummy,' she yelled, 'there's a bald lady at the front door who is asking to speak with you.'

'It will be Soṇā', said a voice from somewhere I later discovered to be the kitchen.

Elise shot into the hall from what was her own room. Whether forbidden or not she rushed forwards and put her arms around me and held me tight.

'How wonderful that you are here, Soṇā. Fiene!' she called out, 'someone so very special is here.'

Fiene came out from the kitchen.

'Ah Soṇā, we've been expecting you,' she said, utterly bewildering the new arrival. 'Come and have some tea and Boterkoek, a Dutch cake even better than your own Dundee cake. You are more than welcome.'

I was feeling totally overwhelmed by my reception. Hearing the noise, Julia and Gale had also come, though primarily to see a lady who was bald!

Once the hurly-burly of my arrival had settled, Elise led me into the study, where I immediately paused to look at the burning candle.

'*Shekinah*', I said.

Elise smiled and we both sat.

'What did your mother-in-law mean when she said you were expecting me? We've communicated only once since you were at Samye Ling, and I said nothing about coming.'

'Of course you did. It was present in every line of your letter. I seemed to know that it would be sometime this week.'

'Elise Westernberg, you are impossible!'

'You'll meet my husband later and he will agree.'

'But how could you know I would come?'

'You told me on the morning of Tomas's death as we drove back in the Land Rover in all that snow. It was clear to me, and I knew it was also clear to you, that you would come to be with your sister!'

'You're not easy to get to. The 8:02 bus from Eskdalemuir to Lockerbie, train to Carlisle and then to Newcastle and then to Northallerton and another bus journey through lower Wensleydale.'

'That's quite a journey in more senses than one and you must be very tired. Your room is ready and waiting, where you can have a shower and a rest. One rucksack suggests you might not have much in the way of a change of clothes, but I'll root out something of mine you can endure until we can go shopping.

'Elise, I'm utterly bewildered.'

'I would imagine you are, so let's leave conversation until we're both up to it. I can imagine the last few days have taken their toll.'

I nodded and followed Elise meekly up the stairs.

When Elise returned from milking her goats on Thursday morning, she found me in the kitchen helping Fiene bake some bread.

'I must have coffee and porridge before anything,' said Elise, 'so I fear you may have to put up with my smelly attire.'

'I have survived so far,' said Fiene, 'and my son often smells even worse.'

After her breakfast, a shower and change of clothes Elise invited me to join her in the study.

'H'm,' said Elise, 'Your slim figure does greater justice to my old clothes than ever they did to me.'

'Although the Buddha is always portrayed as well built, shall we say it would never do for a member of the Sangha to look as if they over-partook.'

'And are you still a member of the Sangha?'

'I'm glad you're beginning with an easy question,' I replied with a laugh, 'though I knew our conversation this morning would be tough, just as my conversation was on the day before yesterday with Rinpoche.'

'Tell me.'

'I told him I needed some time out. At first, he said no, but when I asked again, he reluctantly agreed to a one week break at home with my parents in North Berwick, so here I am with you and your family in Wensleydale. Obedient – that's me! I think he knew he had no choice and that I was going to be on 8:02 bus whatever.

'You see, Elise, it was the moment when you simply said without hesitation that you would come and baptise him that I knew I would have to leave.

'I knew at that moment that the circle was now complete. Yes, it was *Karuṇā*, compassion, but for me necessity was laid upon me, and to have refused would have been the negation of all that had gone before. There were no voices, no lights in the sky, but I knew, in the same way you have come to realise what you have had to do, however painful.'

'When I woke up very early this morning,' said Elise, 'my first thought was of all the potential riches you have brought with you. Nothing need be repudiated or regretted because you carry great treasures with you wherever and whatever you will do, from which

I am eager to benefit.'

'But what am I to do now?'

'Years ago, my spiritual guide, Jean-Pierre, gave me the perfect spiritual instruction. He said that my life should consist of nothing special, that I should just be ordinary. He knew, though, that the ordinary is the special, and that it was in the ordinary that I would come to know how to live. Not that five years in silence was what most people would consider ordinary, nor your own silent retreat of three years and three months and three days.'

'No, they wouldn't.'

'But in a very real sense it was. I had to shed all the theories and ambitions that had characterised my life, my good and bad opinions. It took me five years and a lot of reflecting upon the deaths that I had witnessed, to enable me to learn Jean-Pierre's simple lesson.'

'Meditation on our death is an important Buddhist practice, though you experienced these things not as ideas but in terms of flesh and blood literally in your hands, even on the telephone.'

'You are free to return to Samye Ling after your break,' said Elise, 'and they will welcome you back, but I hope you will remain here in Wensleydale living with us. Pieter said to me last night how much he already liked you and was glad you are going to be here to keep me out of mischief in a sisterly sort of way.

'But Soṇā, in different ways you and I have something that needs to be passed on. I have not felt remotely able to conceive how this could be done until I met you. But I think that as the river down in the valley has been made of different streams, different sources, I want to share the flow with you, and allow it to go on for others to bathe in.'

I was unable to hold back the flow of tears.

'Elise, I know nothing.'

'Then you have just said the magic words which might just make it possible. But my darling, you need a holiday first, so do nothing for a week or two other than get used to the Yorkshire air and accents, and perhaps we can go for walks up the dale together. You're safe here, Soṇā.

'Soon will come the great Jewish celebration of Pesach, Passover, commemorating the Exodus. The story may have no foundation in historical events, but the part of the story I most like is how they set out crossing the Red Sea, knowing nothing about what lay before them.'

'I have already made that crossing, Elise, and I am already safe on the other side. I know I'm happy being here with you and knowing nothing other than *Shekinah*.'

Elise and I smiled at one another.

'I do think,' she said, 'that you should let your mum and dad know you are safe and well. Eventually Rinpoche or someone else may go to their home to discover what has happened when you fail to return to Samye Ling. You mustn't cause them any worry. '

'Thank you, but what am I going to say, and for that matter, Elise, what am I even to think and do? I knew I had to come but for what, other than to be with you? That was the only thought I had and now I'm here, what now?'

'You were not lying when you said you needed a rest, a holiday. So here is the opportunity for you to lie on your bed whenever you choose, eat Fiene's wonderful cooking and come out with me, if you wish, into these wonderful Dales, allowing me to share your company which I have longed for. Since leaving the Waiting Room, now a long time ago, I have rejoiced in the love I know from and with my family, but I have also known a loneliness of spirit. And then I met you at dinnertime in the dining hall and for the first time I was aware that the loneliness had come to an end. It was sealed in what you called *Karuṇā*, the act of love in which we shared, compassion, in that bitterly cold snowy night. And that was why I knew all that has followed. The question of times and seasons of your arrival is best left not worried about, for after all there are more things in Heaven and Earth, Soṇā, than are dreamt of in your Buddhist or my Jewish/Christian philosophy, as our friend the Bard might have written.'

Suddenly all I could do was laugh, and Elise joined me as we tightened hold of one another's hands.

'Tomorrow is market day. Let's go and see what it has to offer,' said Elise.

'But I have no money,' I replied, suddenly struck by the memory of when I made my lifetime commitment and handed every penny over to the Sangha. I told Elise this.

'If you decide not to return, we should perhaps pursue this matter. I'm sure it will have been faced before, but in the meantime, we shall go to the bank in town and open an account for you. I already owe you a great deal and giving you money is simply repayment.'

'I can't accept that,' I said. 'It wouldn't be fair.'

'And it isn't fair that that when my dad died, he left me a fortune, but he did, so here is a chance to make good use of it.'

'Did he really?'

'Yes, he had shares in a Canadian mining company and in monetary terms I am moderately wealthy, though you and I know that true wealth is quite different. And in any case, you are my sister, and we should share my father's money.'

I looked at the candle burning before us.

'*Shekinah*,' I said.

'Oh yes.'

Elise raised my hand to her lips.

'I wish for you only joy.'

'Thank you,' I replied lamely, almost dumbfounded.

Elise gave a gentle laugh.

'Perhaps after lunch we might go for a walk. I'm longing to introduce you to Pen Hill, and I find walking in the countryside often helps clear my thinking. And then tomorrow we can go to the market and open a bank account for you, and even get you a mobile phone. With that you'll be easily accessible to your mum and dad.'

A little later, I sat on chair at the desk in Elise's room and dialled my parent's home number.

'Lizzie?' said my mum. 'Are you ok?'

'Yes. Mum, I'm fine, really fine. But look, I've left Samye Ling.'

'You've done what? Where are you?'

'I'm ok, I promise, so just let me explain. Rinpoche thinks I'm at home with you for a week's break, and it may be that when I don't get back, someone will make contact. Please tell them the truth that I didn't come home if they do make contact. I don't want you to lie to them.'

'But why, and where are you?'

'I'm in the Yorkshire Dales living with the person who's become my closest friend, together with her husband, three children and a Dutch mother. It is the Westernberg family, in which Pieter is the local vet and my friend Elise, has her own flock of goats which she milks every day and, to add to the mix, is a rabbi, or at least she was a very long time ago.'

'Lizzie, please stop, and break this up into bits for me. I'm utterly confused. I thought you had made a life commitment as a nun?'

'And there's nothing about that I can't fulfil out in the wider world.'

'Are you in your robes? They'll look a bit odd in the Yorkshire Dales.'

'Like my haircut you mean? No, I'm wearing some of Elise's clothes and we're going shopping on the market this morning.'

'But what about money? You made it all payable over to the Temple when you took your monastic vow.'

'And I shall have to try and find out how I can recover it – this must have happened before. I just can't remember what the documents said.'

'Dad made copies. But my darling, are you sure this is the right thing to do?'

'Mum, I knew it wasn't right to marry David, and I've known for about six weeks that I had to leave and come here. The money thing Elise and I have sorted. I only arrived yesterday so I haven't really begun to think about the future, but Pieter and Elise want me to stay here.

'The thing is, mum, Elise spent five years in solitude, which is almost two years more than I did but we feel a real spiritual kinship far closer than anything I knew at Samye Ling, wonderful though that was. When I consider the reality of the world as it is, and my own experiences, I've come to the realisation that the language of Buddhism makes considerably less sense to me than once it did, though my spiritual practice of meditation will continue, even if in a form I can't now imagine. But the main thing is that I have made the right decision.'

'Will you be able to come and see us?'

'Of course, but for the present it might be better if you take a trip to Yorkshire. I would love to see you and for you to see me looking almost normal again.'

'And so would we. "Almost" normal did you say? That sounds about right. But whatever, Lizzie, you know we love you so much. Oh, I've had a thought. What are you to be called? Lizzie or Soṇā?'

'Mum, all you need to know is that I'm perfectly safe and happy to be here with lovely people and goats.'

Her mum laughed.

'Oh Lizzie, I shouldn't say this, but I'm so happy. How can we get in touch with you?'

I gave her the phone number though said Elise was suggesting I obtain a mobile and if I did so, I would let her know the number.

'Gosh, you really are joining the real world.'

'No, mum, I never left it. All I have done is altered my way of looking at it, learning to see it differently.'

Market Day

I slept well after our walk up Pen Hill, though I was out of breath a lot of the time. But the climb was worth it because the view from the flat top towards Upper Wensleydale and the Pennines beyond was wonderful. Perhaps the best thing about the walk was that it provided us with the opportunity to let each other know more of our pasts, before the days of what Elise called our "solitary refinement". Mine amounted to considerably less than her own though I already knew from her visit to Samye Ling something of the deaths and tragedies in which she had been closely involved, but the story of how she became a rabbi was new to me and I found it fascinating, not least discovering that she had been, unusually for a woman, a scholar and teacher of Talmud, even if I wasn't exactly sure what it was.

I slept late (for me), showered and dressed and then went down to Elise's room as she had told me to do whenever I wished. I saw first the burning candle, *Shekinah*, and, quite unexpectedly, I thought someone must have followed me into the room and I turned round but there was no one there. For a Buddhist this was, to say the least, disconcerting, no matter how much Elise took it for granted, and for just a moment I shivered.

I looked round the room and was surprised to see far fewer

books than I might have expected given I knew of the scholarship of her early years. I did however see that it contained a number of books whose authors I knew of, most of them relating to mystical experience, the majority from the medieval period. There were some books with Hebrew titles I could not decipher but the overwhelming feel of the room was one of peace. I was about to sit down when the door did open. It was Fiene.

'Elise is still doing the goats but she'll be back soon. Come and have some breakfast. How did you sleep?'

'I can't remember, which suggests it was good and for the first time in many years so comfy in a soft bed. It's very quiet for a house with three children.'

'They all have to leave early for the bus to school. There's no secondary school here, and they're used to getting up early. It's easier for us now Gale has joined Julia and Grace, and they travel together.'

'They are lovely girls, and their names are astonishing. Grace is so appropriate for a couple who have come together as Elise and Pieter have. And Julia must always be a reminder of your first daughter-in-law. And Gale, for Elise the beginning of her encounters with the life of whatever one wants to call it, the woman who took her own life whilst on the phone to her.'

'It is typical of Elise and Pieter that they have chosen special names. And yes, I do remember Julia, Pieter's first wife who died of cancer, though I did not know her well as I was still living in Holland during the brief time of their marriage. She was a lovely girl, but did you know that it was Elise who chose the name?'

'It doesn't surprise me.'

'What doesn't?' said a voice belonging to a body coming into the kitchen to join them.

'That you have big ears!' said Fiene to her daughter-in-law.

'I was speaking of the names of your children, but especially that of Julia. I wondered whether just hearing it might still after so long be painful for Fiene and Pieter.'

'I think for both of us,' said Fiene, 'such pain as once we knew has been transformed. When I say Julia's name I now think only on the most mischievous of my three grandchildren, but my smelly daughter who has just joined us has always insisted that the lovely photograph of the original Julia should still be kept in place in the sitting room.'

'Of course. The past is always there to nourish us, as roots feed the flower.'

'Thank you for your thought for the day, Elise! My piece of wisdom is that you need to change your clothes, or the kitchen will smell of goats.'

'Oh mama, I'm wasted on you!' said Elise with a huge grin as she looked at me, before departing.

I sat at the table, where there were fresh warm croissants, something I hadn't eaten for years, and with apricot conserve they were as good as they were smelling.

Elise joined us and said, 'It's market day, and we have things to do. To open a bank account and buy a phone will require you to give your full name,' said Elise. 'But I don't think you should rush into any sort of decision about that – or at least not until we go shopping.'

'Gee, thanks for that.'

Elise and Fiene laughed.

I mentioned to Elise that I was feeling guilty about not having spent time in meditation, but she told me that I was on my holidays and there would be plenty of time for us both to speak together of such things.

'The most important thing you need now is to fling off outward obligation and enjoy the wonder of the Dales and life in your new family, doing whatever you want, reading what you want. That is what a holiday is meant to do, and it can last just as long as you wish it to. And, yes, in time we can talk over the things we need to do, but not on market day.'

She said no more.

I had a surprise at the bank, when the senior assistant (who, as seemingly with everyone else in the town, knew Elise well) looked at to her computer and after a search found that I still had a bank account with them (or at least their Scottish branch) containing £72 – the effect of interest – and so did not need to open a new account. Then to my astonishment, Elise paid £5,000 into the account, allowing the bank to order bank cards which would come within within five working days. Elizabeth McKenzie it seemed, was officially alive again!

Elise suggested I withdraw some cash to enable me to buy something for myself on the market, which by now was already busy, but before that we went to a shop selling mobile phones and Elise paid for a basic pay-as-you-go Nokia which I gazed upon in wonder and fear! I had seen many people at Samye Ling using them but had never done so myself. Elise said that the best person to teach her to use it would be Grace when she got back from school!

I loved the market and all the people there who seemed full of life as they wandered from stall to stall. Elise bought some veg and fruit whilst I looked at the clothes on offer and came away with a pair of jeans, two shirts and a jumper, and of course, as we are women, Elise insisted on me showing her them as we stopped for a coffee. She approved!

On the way back home, she mentioned that Aishe was hoping to call in for some lunch. She had come with Elise and Leah to Samye Ling and was the one of the three I knew least, but I did know that since her visit she had been in regular contact with one of the meditation teachers at the Temple, Martha Murray, whom I knew well, so I looked forward to meeting her.

I at once changed into my new jeans and shirt and looked at myself in the mirror, and catching sight of my bald head, wondered just who I was. I was summoned by Fiene to a phone call from my mum.

'Hello, my darling. How are you doing this morning, though who was that wonderful person I've just been speaking to?'

'That was Fiene, the Dutch mother of Pieter and Elise's adopted mother who lives here and is indeed very special. But I'm really fine.'

I told her about the bank account and that I now had a mobile telephone, gave her the number but said I would need the help of one of Elise's teenage children later in the day to learn how to work it!

'And I've bought myself some new clothes on the market – make sure when you come you include a Friday as you would love the market.

'Oh, Lizzie, I can't tell you how wonderful it is to hear you talking about the ordinary things of life. What are you going to do about your hair and what about your name?'

'Well, these are good questions. For now, I'm a Buddhist nun on holiday and here they call me Soṇā, which is how Elise has known me from the first. I need time to consider lots of things, but it will be greatly helped when you two can drive down the A1 or get the train and come to stay.'

'Where would we stay?'

'That's not a problem, just give me times and dates.'

'Oh Lizzie, I am so happy for you, and for me and your dad. Please thank Fiene for being so lovely and tell her I am looking forward to meeting her, and of course to meeting Elise.'

'So,' said Fiene, as I entered the kitchen to show off my new clothes, 'when are they coming to see this new lady before me in such a lovely blouse and jeans?'

'I've urged them to come as soon as possible as it will help me to think about the future. Once I find out, perhaps you will recommend a B&B.'

'They will do all their feeding here, I hope. In terms of rooms we're now full, unless their daughter is willing to share a room with Grace. There's a spare single bed in her room but you will have to ask her.'

'I'm hoping she will help me work my mobile telephone.'

'She will love that, but we just call them mobiles!'

At that moment the doorbell rang. It was Aishe, and into the kitchen came the most beautiful Indian-looking woman I have ever seen.

Aishe

I had only briefly met Aishe on her visit with Leah and Elise to Samye Ling, so hadn't quite been ready to see how simply beautiful she is. Elise told me she worked as a speech therapist, had a son, Raj, married to Tan, one of the doctors in the town, and was of course Welsh! She was the daughter of East African Asians who had been forced from their homes by General Amin and come to live in Britain, in their case in Wales, where she had met another East African Asian and married

As we ate our lunch, I noticed that all the food prepared for me since my arrival had been vegetarian, including this one, and I felt I ought to say something to Fiene about this. I did not want the household to change its way of doing things just for me and I had seen different sorts of meat in the fridge, but as with the question of my name, I had to give thought to the question of how much of Buddhist practice I had to bring with me to sustain the reality of my continuing as a Buddhist nun. Already I had shed my robes but having only shaved my head less than a week earlier I was still bald. Would I now let it grow? I decided to raise this now with Aishe, Fiene and Elise as we sat together.

'How many components can you remove from a car for it still to be a car?' I asked.

The others seemed taken aback by what was wholly

incongruous in the context of the things we had been discussing. I could see at once, however, that Elise guessed what I was saying.

'I assume you are talking about yourself.'

I smiled.

'Yes, I am talking about me, and my experiences at the bank and obtaining a phone, but above all my conversations with my mum, are making me think hard. For example, you seem to be providing vegetarian food for me but here I am in the house of those who work with farm animals in a farming community where they will want to eat to support those around them.

'I've been doing vegetarian food because beginning to eat meat again, if that's what you choose, will take your insides some adjusting to,' said Fiene, 'but if you want to eat only vegetarian food then I will happily prepare that for you.'

'Well, there you are,' I said with a large smile, 'already you have helped me decide. In the face of such generosity and kindness I cannot ask that of you. I will eat what you eat.'

'Perhaps you can begin with fish.'

I nodded, tears in my eyes.

'You only arrived here two days ago,' added Elise, 'and I would suggest we need more time before you feel confident about any decision you may choose to make. But I don't think any of us doubt your complete integrity and profound wisdom about the things that matter to you. The most important thing for now is that you are on holiday, and you can relax your rigorous discipline, even if just for a while.'

After lunch, Aishe and I sat for a while in Elise's room whilst she paid a visit to the cattle and sheep market in the town. It was part of her support for Pieter's work in maintaining contacts and reminding farmers and their wives that their vet cared for them and should not allow things to get out of hand before calling him. In fact, as I was to discover, he was widely trusted in the community, not least because of the work she did in keeping the network operating.

'As you know,' said Aishe, as we sat with our post-dinner mugs of tea, 'when I came to Samye Ling, I was able to meet with Martha Murray and she helped me greatly as I set about what I suppose were the basics of meditation and she suggested some books to read and reflect upon as I maintained daily practice. I talked this over with Elise and confessed that although meditation made sense, hardly any of the Buddhist ideology that came in the package did so.

'Elise speaks about the difference between belief and knowing, that what someone claims they believe, even passionately, does not prove the truth of what they claim. Buddhism comes with a hefty package of beliefs as I have discovered, some of them quite bizarre. Each day I engage in meditation in the ways Martha has instructed me, but something has caused me to think about what I am doing in a different way.

'My husband and I were brought up as non-practising Hindus, by parents themselves also non-practising, and that is how we are bringing up our own son. But by doing some exploring into what I might call my spiritual DNA, I came across a Catholic priest and monk called Henri le Saux who, out in India, began to explore the Hindu practice of prayer and gave himself over to this. He adopted Hindu dress, accepted guidance from a Hindu guru, formed an ashram and became known as Abishikeśvarānda which means "Bliss of the Anointed One", though is better known as Swami Abhishiktānanda. He continued to speak of himself as a Christian Hindu and though he hoped his life there might be followed up by others, it has not proved to be the case.

'On the second-hand book stall on the market, shortly after I returned from Samye Ling, I found a small book by him, simply entitled "Prayer", which cost me 5p. I read it in one sitting and was simply bowled over, not so much by the Christian content, but by the way he introduced me to my own past and what is still a living tradition. Elise has encouraged me to pursue this and day by day I am discovering it is speaking to my heart in ways the Buddhism of Martha simply does not.'

'Then I think you should trust Elise, but even more to trust your own intuitive sense that this is right, and what a voyage of discovery this may prove to be for you. I recall my own limited experience of the far north of India when I went to see Kanchenjunga. In Darjeeling I was aware that in addition to the many Hindu shrines and their activities there was also a living spiritual tradition centred on meditation or prayer, though I had little time, nor at that stage an inclination to know more about it.'

'Abhishiktānanda calls the practice of meditation or prayer dhyāna, but he also wrote much about silence and though never having given himself to it in the way you and Elise have done, more and more of his later writing speaks of its necessity. I fear that his Christian origins continued to exercise a hold upon him and much of that means nothing to me, and in any case seems utterly unrelated to what Christianity as I see it is about. It remains "poor little talkative Christianity" as EM Forster described it in *A Passage to India*.

'Perhaps you and I,' continued Aishe, 'can talk further about this, but thinking back to the issues you are facing, they are not wholly different from those Elise faced when she abandoned the rabbinate, and discovered she had to let go of everything if she was going to engage fully with the spiritual task set her by Fr Jean-Pierre at the time of her return visit to Canada. To endeavour to make sense of the suffering she had known, and not least the reality of the Holocaust, she only discovered the reality of what this candle before us signifies, *Skekinah,* the Presence.

'What I think I am saying, and you must take no notice of it as I am not in the same league as a warrior of the spirit as you, is that shedding is not defeat, is not failure but may be the necessary next stage, just as a cygnet has to shed its early feathers in order to become a swan, and it is usually about 4 years before it becomes an independent adult, and that would be true of all birds, I imagine.'

I laughed.

'I take it you are thinking me to be an ugly duckling!' I said with a laugh.

'Oh, no. You are a swan – of that I have no doubts, but still with some cygnet feathers possibly.'

'Oh Aishe, I'm already feeling out of my depth compared with the grace and wisdom I am receiving from you, Elise and Fiene.'

'I don't think swans can get out of their depth, and whatever you now choose to shed might only be incidentals or accidentals, if you take my meaning. Religions, I have noticed, have a habit over literally thousands of years of picking up bits and pieces like a magpie, and then declare them essential. You are who you are, and nothing can take away what you already know, and I have every reason to think that you will continue to be there for others, not least myself, to benefit from. What does your name matter to those able to learn so much from you? Or your haircut, for that matter? As for your name, it will depend on whether you are intending to teach meditation and want to use the exotic Soṇā or the Lizzie who in any case is Soṇā. But please forgive me if I'm being insensitive. They are just my Hindu thoughts!'

We both laughed as the door opened and in came Elise, fresh from chatting up the farmers.

'Your laughter sounds good. In my years of solitude, I did laugh a great deal, not least when I was milking cows. It kept me sane.'

'We've been talking about the transformation of cygnets into swans,' said Aishe, 'and the opportunity life presents for shedding unnecessary feathers.'

'That's much too cryptic for me,' said Elise, 'but might you possibly have been continuing the conversation at lunch?'

'Yes,' I said. 'Aishe has been reminding me of how much of your Judaism you had to leave behind when you began your five years of solitude in order to do what now lay before you and hinting that it might be safe to exuviate some of what Soṇā is carrying without losing the essence.'

'Aishe! I've warned you before about using big words!'

We all laughed.

'I was reporting my own feeling that I should let go of Buddhist theory and explore my own Hindu inheritance, as I continue my meditation practice,' said Aishe.

'And have you been able to resolve those issues?' Elise asked me. The most important will take time, perhaps quite a long time, and there is no need to rush, but when your mum and dad come, we shall run into difficulties over what you are called, and we might all end up very confused, you not the least. I think Elizabeth McKenzie is a beautiful name, and if you choose to be known as Lizzie by all those who love you, nevertheless you will still also be Bahuputtika Soṇā. I am Elise *Mary*, don't forget, because it was given me by Jean-Pierre at my baptism as a Catholic.'

'Then I am Elizabeth Soṇā McKenzie, known as Lizzie.'

Elise and Aishe both reached out a hand to me and grinned.

'In which case, Lizzie, it's time for us to have a cup of tea and a piece of Dutch cake.'

'If I had known that was the reward, I would have made the decision sooner!'

We laughed and headed towards the kitchen!

A Yow With Broken Leg

Later, as the whole family gathered for the evening meal, I was astonished to see candles lit as if it was the traditional Jewish Friday evening ceremony marking the beginning of Shabbat, and then I remembered that at this table along with Pieter, Fiene and myself, the other four persons present were Jewish. It was Julia who took the cup of wine, held it high with the words "The cup of Blessing", and then each of us drank from it. Then Gale did the same with a pitta bread, and each of us broke a little and ate it. That was it. No other ceremonial words were used and to my eyes it seemed as if the girls took this as a natural part of what they did on Fridays. It was so simple and delightful, and to my further joy they accepted my change of name with ease.

Elise explained to me later that although what had taken place was quite different from the full Jewish Friday evening meal, it was a simple way for her and the children to remember that they were Jewish, though she did point out that they did not actually keep Saturday as Jews do Shabbat.

Grace, true to her name had expressed herself more than willing to allow me to sleep in her room when my mum and dad came. She also gave me lessons on how use my mobile to make calls and send texts, and shortly after leaving the table it suddenly burst into life, almost terrifying me. It was my dad.

'Lizzie, is that really you?'

I burst into tears and struggled to say, 'Yes, dad.'

Elise indicated I should go to her room so we could speak in private.

'Most important of all, Lizzie, are you ok, are you safe?'

'Oh yes, dad, I truly am and happy to be here with friends who have welcomed me into their home and indeed into their life, and are very much hoping, as I am, that you will soon be able to come and stay here.'

'We're going to come on Wednesday, if that's alright with you. We'll drive down as that will give us the chance to take you out and explore Yorkshire.'

'That would be fabulous, and Pieter and Elise want you to stay here.'

'I haven't done anything yet about the money you paid Samye Ling when you were ordained, because I didn't want to let them know that you had left until you were ready to tell them yourself.'

'Thanks, dad, and how is everyone, Mike and Pauline and their families?'

'We're all so delighted to know that you are where you are and with those who can support and care for you. We'll have the opportunity to fill in details when we come.'

'Oh, dad, I can't wait to see you, though you should know that I'm in unusual clothes: jeans, shirt and jumper'

'I've never seen you in jeans before! Oh Lizzie, mum and I are so looking forward to being with you. We're planning to leave early and should be with you by lunchtime.'

'*Dinner*time, dad. This is Yorkshire!'

Although Saturday was not kept with Shabbat discipline, it was regarded very much as a family day. Elise drove the three girls to Richmond to do some shopping, Fiene only provided food prepared earlier and Pieter unwound completely, living always in the hope that the phone did not summon him to an animal in need. But just before noon, he received a call to attend a sheep that might have a broken leg. He asked me if I would like to go with him and I jumped at the chance, not to see the yow (as they are known) but for the chance to spend time with Pieter.

He is not a tall man but exceptionally strong and clearly very patient living with a mother, a wife, three daughters and now a former nun, though I can tell he enjoys the female company as a contrast to the smelly men, cows and yows his days are taken up with. His definite Yorkshire accent also contained a very definite Dutch element which was very attractive. Elise had told me that farmers' wives loved him, and I could understand why.

'I'm looking forward to your mum and dad coming,' he said as we set off in his van which to my eyes contained a veritable chemist shop of drugs and equipment. 'How long is it since you last saw them?'

'About a year, I suppose. They always came for my birthday.'

'And was it easy for them, you becoming a Buddhist nun?'

'I imagine that having a brother and sister who have children, giving them grandchildren, they could more easily allow me to do something daft.'

'Do they think it was daft?'

'If you could hear the excitement in their voices on my last two calls, you would know the answer to that. But however daft, they thought it, they always gave their support and love.'

'A long time back, when I first met Elise when we were together testing cows for TB, although she told me all about her five years of solitary refinement, as she calls it which took some getting round in my mind, I never thought she was daft. In fact, it was her lack of daftness, and her reluctance to speak of it even to me, that most convinced me that I had to rethink completely my own previous dismissal of anything even remotely religious. I did wonder when Elise announced that a Buddhist nun was coming whether you might be daft, but you're so like Elise in many ways, and again it's what you don't say that most impresses me.'

'I'm trying to get my mind round that, but I think it's meant to be a compliment.'

'She's never said in so many words, but I know that despite our family life which is as wonderful as it seems, and all the people she knows and know her, she is lonely at, what for want of a better word, the spiritual level or, better still the silent level. I share her awareness of *Shekinah*, but not in the way she does, because I think she doesn't just think it, she feels it. Does that make sense?'

'You are married to an exceptional person, Pieter, and I know how much she adores you, and did so literally from day one when you met on the farm, so what you say makes good sense to me. Since meeting her and sharing in the death of a tiny new-born baby when she did something special, I have also felt acute loneliness, which is why I've come here.'

He turned into a gateway and then into a farmyard.

'Well, come and see why I've come here,' he said.

It didn't take him long to see that the bone was broken but not so badly that the yow would need to be put down. From the van he produced bandages which he put into a bucket of water the farmer had ready prepared, and these turned into a plaster with which he skilfully wrapped the leg of the yow who, once he had released her, ran off much less impressed than me.

'I take it she hasn't been tupped yet?' said Peter to the farmer, 'as I know you prefer late tupping and lambing. She should mend in about 4-6 weeks' time, but the leg will be ok if she gets tupped before then.'

'Thanks Pieter, and is this your new assistant?'

'Lizzie's staying with us for a while. She's a very special family friend and fancied a trip out with me.'

'There's a batch of newly baked sausage rolls in the kitchen. Bella will be pleased to see you.'

Ah, I thought to myself, the test!

I walked into the kitchen and met Bella and her two teenage sons who were sprawling on a sofa and doing not a lot, but who waved and greeted Pieter. She gave us mugs of tea and the smell of the freshly baked sausage rolls entranced me and so for the first time in many years I bit into and swallowed meat – and it was wonderful. I have no idea what the nectar of the gods was like, but it cannot have been better than this! Seeing my pleasure, Bella said she'd put some others into a bag for us to take home. Quite honestly, I could have eaten the lot there and then! I hoped that this was not one of the incidentals mentioned by Aishe that I could shed on my way to full swanhood!

'Are farmers good payers?' I asked Pieter on our way back.

'He is,' he replied, 'but not everyone, by any means. Sometimes Elise pays a visit with an up-to-date invoice and she charms the payments out of them, but as we say Holland, "bloed uit een steen halen". I suspect you can work out the meaning!'

'Perhaps I should send Elise to Samye Ling. When I joined I had to hand over all my worldly goods, meaning the contents of all my bank and saving accounts which were quite a lot. One of the things my dad is going to investigate is how, if at all, we can get the money back now I have left.'

'Having left, are you still bound by vows and things?'

'It's ok, Pieter, I'm going to let my hair grow!'

He laughed.

'It's up to me. I will have broken my vows, and if my leave is permanent I will in essence be cast out. But what can't be cast out is all that I have lived, known and experienced as a Buddhist nun. As for the finances. They are controlled by lay stewards rather than the Sangha itself, and they are ones my dad will have to contact. I've met them and they are good people, but we shall see what rules they are bound by. But clearly, if all else fails, I will send Elise.'

At dinner time the rest of the sausage rolls were quickly dealt with. I did confess to having eaten and thoroughly enjoyed one earlier which caused great amusement.

'Does that mean you can eat what I would wish to prepare for your mum and dad coming?' said Fiene.

'I'm not sure I could manage offal or rare steaks, but yes, provided it's as good as Bella's sausages!'

Everyone laughed.

For the rest of the day, I acquired the wonderful art of lying on a comfortable bed, reading a book suggested by Elise called *Olivia Doyle* – mostly set in the Dales not so far from where we were, and so different from anything I had read in many years that it was the equivalent in paper and ink to the sausage roll of my morning farm visit.

On the Saturday evening the great treat was what in Scotland we call a "fish supper" but here was simply fish and chips from the shop in town, brought by Grace and Julia, with something called mushy peas, to which I gave my undivided attention.

Before going to bed, Elise asked if I would like to go with her in the morning over to her old waiting room on the North York coast.

'I just thought you might like to see it. I probably can't get to Holy Isle, but I'd love to share it with you.'

'Do you still own it?'

'Yes, but in summer we let it as a holiday house. Anyway, it means early start and once I've milked the goats, Julia's going to do the dairy work for me, so we can set off by about 8-00. OK?'

'It will be a great privilege for me to see such a special place, but now I have a date in bed with a poet called Olivia Doyle.'

A Journey

'The goats gave me a very old-fashioned look when I went so very early this morning, but as always it didn't stop them wanting their food which allows me to milk them. But it allows us quiet roads at this time of the day.'

'Do you go back to the house often?'

'No. The local farmer's wife keeps an eye on the place and does the cleaning and washing between the lets, but I like to go over and see her. How much longer they'll be there I don't know as they're getting into their 70s and farming's not easy at that age.'

The roads were quiet as we crossed the A1 and headed up on the North York Moors via the steep Sutton Bank.

'Why did you choose up here?' I asked Elise.

'I didn't; it chose me. I heard on the radio that the RAF were selling it and I made an immediate offer by phone even before it was advertised and bought it even without seeing it. There was a lot of work to be done when I arrived and I had next to no furniture but I paid a visit to some of the second-hand stores in Malton, though I did buy a proper bed. And when I arrived, I knew at once it was the right place for me. It can be very cold, but I come from Canada, which is much colder in winter, and you grew up adjacent to the North Sea and its winds, so you know what I mean.'

'This is the first chance we've had to be together properly since

I arrived. I'm still dumbstruck by your knowledge of my coming.'

'Don't be. It wasn't magic of any kind so much as intuition arising from what we shared on that night. I couldn't come to be with you, so it would have to be the other way round. I hope you're not regretting it. In theory you could return by Wednesday, and no one would be any the wiser.'

'I would and you would, and how would you explain it to my mum and dad', I said with a smile. 'I'm hoping to convince them that I'm not as mad as the whole family have always assumed, and were they to find me gone, well, I can't imagine what they would think. But the question above all that they are going to ask, and somewhere inside myself I am asking it too – what now?'

'That's the obvious question they will ask, but for you and me it's the wrong one, though I'm not sure yet what the right question is, and I think we shall need to be patient. All we know so far is that we are meant to be together, and that is enough to be going on with.'

'Ok, and I know that's right, but I have some questions to ask which we've never really had the chance to consider. The first is about practice, yours and mine. The second is what *Shekinah* means to you. I had an odd experience entering your room the other day. I could have sworn I wasn't alone, that someone had followed me in but when I turned there was no one there.'

'That's such a relief,' answered Elise. 'No one else has ever said that and I've often felt it must be my over-active imagination at work.'

'It didn't feel as if I might have been imagining it, it seemed much more tangible, well, not tangible as such, but real, as if there was almost a movement of air.'

'That's it exactly – like a movement of air.'

'But what is it?'

'I've no idea and I would suggest it's important neither of us attempts to make sense of it, because whatever we might say or think would inevitably be wrong. I return to my old philosopher friend Ludwig Wittgenstein's "whereof one cannot speak, one must be silent."'

'The thing is though, and I had to face this in becoming a Buddhist, I don't believe in God.'

'Nor me, but tell me about the god you don't believe in. Are you referring to the gods that Tibetan Buddhists in particular believe inhabit the existence faced after death, together with hungry ghosts and even more? I know that's what Aishe has found impossible with what she has been asked to read by Martha Murray.'

'It's most odd,' I replied. 'Some of those who come to Samye Ling inhabit worlds of scientific and technological reality, and many are highly intelligent, and yet for whatever reason they come to believe in what is honestly simply a reflection of the beliefs of Tibetans and Nepalese as far back as 2,300 years ago. I understand of course that ideas, per se, take form and expression in tangible form within communities. What all the religions of the world don't seem to have grasped is that those tangible expressions come to predominate and become necessary, and the more they are passed on, the more unquestionable they become, and end up as the *sine qua non* of that tradition. Aishe will discover that in Hinduism and were she to attend a temple ceremony might wonder what it has to do with the mystical tradition she is discovering.

'It is the same for Christianity. Catholicism is caught in not wanting to deny that the accretions of centuries are essential to the faith but say something to a world so radically different. The Reformation was an attempt to do that, I suppose, but Protestantism is not immune to historical drag either.'

'Strangely enough, Judaism, apart from the Hasid who seek still to inhabit 18th century Poland, has proved remarkably adept at changing its forms and expressions though there are still tensions between Orthodox and Reform.'

'What were you?'

'Not were, I *am* a Reform rabbi still, even though most of my fellow Jews would think me well beyond the pale and already in the realm of hungry ghosts!'

I laughed.

'But we have lived through the Shoah from which we continue to learn a great deal if we can keep it in mind, and I continue to live with all the deaths and tragedies I have lived through too, but I would love to hear about the god you cannot or don't believe in.'

'I was hoping to avoid that question,' I said, mischievously, 'but I'm happy to share everything with you, Elise. For me the language of theism, the positing of something, someone, however metaphorically up in the sky, belongs to a past best forgotten. It is a series of beliefs simply reflecting the human structures that gave them birth. The gods of popular belief arise primarily from the psychological longings we all have for the welfare of ourselves and others, and the recognition that in this world as we grow up there are no mummies and daddies to make everything ok. That is understandable. But then some people need to systematise it and do so imitating the world's political structures, in the widest sense of the word, in that there are those at the top and those below them and below them and so on. The top god becomes King and Lord, Mighty and All-Knowing, and of course it was always a male god, and below him, angels and the like, as human potentates had their servants to do their will.

'Sometimes there were those who spoke of this god as loving and caring, a god who occasionally intervenes in response to our pleading, but such a belief is possible only to those who know nothing of history and are deliberately blind to the realities of living and dying now.

'So, for me, the gods of Ancient Greece and Rome, which no one believes in now, are exactly the same as the god of Judaism and Christianity, the gods of Hinduism and Islam and so very many more religions, and I include those of Tibetan and Nepalese Buddhism.'

'Have you ever heard of Etty Hillesum?'

'No.'

'She is becoming an important part of my life through her diary which she wrote between 1941-1943. She was a Dutch Jew, gassed as her parents shortly before her, in Auschwitz on 30 November 1943, aged 29. I only found out about her when we were in Holland last year for our annual holiday and there was an exhibition about her in Utrecht. She was not a religious Jew in terms of practice but came to what I can only describe as a mystical sense which although she does use the G word, is about as far from the theism you and I know to be nonsense, and through this sense chose to go to the camps with her people, knowing there would be no divine intervention to save her, but never denied what she knew. It seems to me she embodied what you call *Karuṇā*, compassion.

'How odd for you that you are married to a Dutchman and have an adopted Dutch mother.'

'Oh, Lizzie, my darling, I have learned to live with such oddities and simply welcome rather than question them or give them titles such as "meant to be". Such things happen. That night when the poor little baby died after I had baptised him brought us together. It happened. If it was "meant to be", what sort of meaning in the universe would that be proclaiming, for it would mean accepting that the baby also was meant to die? I do not look for meaning beyond the fact that you and I have become soul-sisters, a term I have never used for any since I parted from my soul-father, Jean-Pierre.'

'And Elise, you avoided the question I asked about *Shekinah*.'

'You had already answered it yourself when you described it a movement of air. As far as my reading goes, I do not think that Etty lost her awareness of God even as she entered the baths to be gassed, nor for that matter did she cease striving to love even those killing her. A movement of air has to be enough. I have so much to learn from you, and it is why we are together.'

The rest of the journey passed in silence and soon we were heading out towards the cliffs but before going to the house, Elise stopped and took me into the farmhouse to meet her very special friends, Jim and Audrey, the only people she had spoken to in her five years alone. They were overjoyed to see her, though Jim looked at the clock on the mantelpiece and pointed that Elise was late for the milking!

'I shall never forget all you both gave me, and not least the vet who came to do the TB testing.'

'How is Pieter?'

'He's well and concentrates on large animals, leaving the cats and dogs to his partners.'

'And what about his lovely mum, whom we met at your wedding?' asked Audrey.

'Fiene is getting older and feels it but continues to cook superbly and is the perfect oma to our children and mama to Pieter and me.'

After some discussion about the house and what should possibly be attended to before the next holiday guests next year and providing us with eggs and milk with which to return to Wensleydale, we left them and walked up to Eastmoor, as it was known, the house that contained the Waiting Room.

Elise opened the door, and we went in.

It was just ordinary, a place where a small family or just a couple might come to enjoy the birds and the sea, what is sometimes called a holiday cottage. None of those who came to stay here could possibly have known of the five-year history of the house between its abandonment by the RAF and its later use for holidays. But of course it was just ordinary, as my own place of solitude had been. Elise had told me Jean-Pierre had stressed the ordinariness of her life and that it was within the ordinary that the holy had to be known and lived. And this house on the edge of the country was the embodiment of ordinariness, and yet I felt I was in a holy place, especially when Elise showed me the small room, now used as a storeroom in which she had spent at least four hours in total silence each day.

'What do you feel when you come in here?' I asked her.

'I recognise it as the storeroom it has been since the day when I knew I had to leave and met Pieter. I admit to a small measure of affection for all that it taught me, in much the way we might feel affection for a former teacher from our schooldays, but I never hated being in there. In fact, more often than not I longed to be in there.'

'Would you call it a time of revelation?'

'I don't give names to what I can't. Besides which, all sorts of supposed revelations are claimed by people, and most of them are simply ridiculous. I take notice of what you say because you waited three years and three months and three days in silence. That is being serious about what you were living.'

'I haven't met my own version of your Pieter yet.'

'Would you like to?'

'My relationship with David did not exactly thrill me in the way I can see yours with Pieter's does, but all we know is that we have come together, and I assume we must wait.'

'In *East Coker*, Eliot wrote:
"I said to my soul, be still, and wait without hope
For hope would be hope for the wrong thing; wait without love
For love would be love of the wrong thing; there is yet faith
But the faith and the love and the hope are all in the waiting."

'I think I held on to those words more than any other when I was here, that they were a promise.'

'However did he write as he wrote? The *Four Quartets* are not much read now, much too spiritual for the present tranche of religion-hating poetry experts.'

'Yes,' replied Elise. 'Jean-Pierre used to say Eliot knew things despite a banal outward life, but I am grateful, and that's all I need to know.'

As we walked back down the lane to collect the car, I felt I had to thank Elise for allowing me into her holy of holies.

'The storeroom you mean. It strikes me that in the history of human encounters with the divine we want to hold on to locations as if they mattered. The holy came with me and has remained with me.'

I was almost thunderstruck by her words and decided to shut up and enjoy the scenery! We would need much more conversation, but I wasn't sure I could engage in any more today, and on the way back I mostly talked about my family, and realised in doing so, just how much I was looking forward to seeing mum and dad again, and this time not as a saffron-robed person from a far distant era.

A Visitation

Poor old mum and dad, I thought, as I eagerly awaited their arrival on the Wednesday morning. They had come out to Nepal to visit me, they had come to see me at Samye Ling, a bizarrely attired, bald Buddhist nun, and now they were travelling down the A1 to meet their daughter once again in an unexpected place. I only hoped that this time they would be meeting the Lizzie they had brought into the world, loved and continued to love wherever and whatever I had done.

I was still on holiday and from the following day "absent without leave" from Samye Ling and I wondered what efforts they might begin making to find me. It raised for me the important question about finding a new lifestyle in which I could return to my meditation practice, which I was beginning to miss, as a musician might begin to feel when separated from their instrument. But this would have to wait.

I saw the car from the window in Elise's room and ran out to meet them and directed them to the parking area for the surgery. I was almost as overwhelmed seeing them as they clearly were at seeing the Lizzie who had been concealed for quite a few years. We hugged and kissed for ages and could barely speak in our excitement. Eventually, dad and I carrying luggage, we went back into the road and along to the front door inside which was a welcoming entourage of Fiene and Elise, by which time mum and dad must have been quite dizzy. Typically, Fiene knew what was needed.

'Put your bags down and come into the kitchen and have a cup of tea and some Dutch cake,' she said, and I could see their eyes light up, though both also expressed a wish to "pay a visit" as my dad put it politely!

It was clear that Fiene intended taking care of this visit and being nearer their age recognised that one of the things they might first need to do after their dinner, was to go to their room and relax for a little while. Dad certainly did, having done all the driving, but mum wanted time with me.

'What a lovely place to be,' she began, 'but you always choose lovely places, though the journey here was not quite as frightening as that to Hilepani. Do you think your journeying days are over now you're here and what are you going to do here? You won't forget you have an excellent degree and are a trained teacher,' she said, in motherly fashion, to which I laughed.

'You didn't say that when I went to Samye Ling and became a nun.'

'Well, to be honest, I didn't really know what to say then. You were entering a world I knew nothing of, but are you still a nun in plain clothes with a bald head?'

'Oh mum, you are funny. To use your words, "to be honest" I have no idea what I might be other than Lizzie McKenzie, though for the moment at least I'm retaining Soṇā as a sort of middle name. Obviously I'm not living as a nun and I imagine I will be cast out of the order, but I continue to bring with me my Buddhist experience even though it may not necessarily appear like that to those who see me, at least what that will look like once my hair has grown.'

She smiled.

'What a lovely lady Fiene is and what you all called dinner was a real treat after that journey. If she feeds you like that you will put a lot of weight on. She told me that she is descended from the Breughels, the great Renaissance painters, and that her late husband was an art expert. And I am very much looking forward later to meeting her son, who I gather is out somewhere in the dale testing cattle.'

'Yes, he loves large animal work and leaves the smaller stuff to his two colleagues.'

'With you and Fiene talking so much, Elise didn't get much chance to speak, but oh, what an astonishingly lovely speaking voice she has.'

'What you heard in the voice is true to the person, trust me, and I know how much she is looking forward to spending time with you and dad, but I want to hear your news, all about the family and life in North Berwick.'

Mum obliged almost without taking a breath for at least half an hour, filling me in with happenings almost since I had entered Samye Ling. I began to feel rather ashamed that I had not known these things, because this was my own family story and I had stayed away from it. I had not seen my brother or sister for a long time, and have nephews and nieces I didn't know, and realised I wanted to put that right.

When dad joined us, I suggested we have a wander round the town though in all honesty at this time of the year, other than a Friday market day, there's not a great deal to see but, wonder of wonders, my bank card had arrived that morning and I was able to buy them a cup of tea in one of the tea shops. My mum, who always was a noticing sort of person with beady eyes, saw the name on the card and expressed delight.

'It wasn't that we didn't want you to become a nun, because we have only wanted you to be happy in whatever you did,' she explained, 'but please excuse our relief at seeing you back in the normal run of the world, though I think we both know that you're not going to disown the best of your past.'

'We did find being totally cut off from you for over three years so very hard,' added dad, 'and you've told us Elise lived alone for five years. I guess both of you must have the sort of inner stamina that few others can manage.'

'Or utterly crackers!' I replied. 'I can't believe that at some time that thought had not crossed your minds.'

Mum and dad gave each other the briefest of glances and I immediately began to laugh.

'You did, didn't you?'

'You must admit that it is not a normal thing to do,' said dad.

'Well put it to the test. Spend some time with Elise and see if you don't find her to be the most normal and well-balanced person you could possibly know.'

'And you are too,' added mum. 'I guess it was only when we spoke of you to others and saw their faces, that we might have wondered.'

'Do those other faces include Mike and Pauline?'

'Of course, but if we can get you to pay a visit home, they can see for yourself.'

'I will come and hopefully soon, maybe even for Christmas, but I've only been away from the monastery for a week, and I need time to readjust both to normal life, as you put it, but also to spend time with Elise who played the key part in my decision to leave. We've hardly had time to think what working together will mean, but what, how and where, I don't know.'

'Did Elise ask you to leave?'

'No. She and I played a part in the middle of a snowstorm when I asked her to come to a young couple whose baby was clearly going to die. I knew that although Elise is Jewish, as a tiny baby herself she had been baptised as a Catholic. I also knew that only one who has been baptised as a Christian can baptise another. There was no time to summon a minister, and so she came and baptised the wee boy shortly before he died in his mother's arms.

'Elise and her two friends were due to return home from Samye Ling on the following day, and other than a short letter I wrote to her, there was no further communication between us until I arrived last Wednesday, though what's really odd is that she had told everyone that I would be coming, and Fiene actually greeted me by name.

'What she did for that baby made me realise that the sort of compassion Buddhists talk about as the aim of all they are about was completely revealed in that amazing act of love, which she accepted in an instant. It turned my world upside down and I felt that this is where I should come. So, I did and here I am.'

'What an amazing story, and a Jewish Catholic who spent five years living in almost total isolation and silence!' said dad. 'And yet here she is in her 50s with a husband and three daughters which is about as normal as anyone could imagine.'

'Not totally normal,' I responded with a grin. 'She also has goats which she milks every day, as you will notice from the aroma when she comes in to breakfast each morning! Until recently she used to go three mornings a week to a local farm to help milk the cows.'

Their eyes widened incredulously.

'I'm sure she'd let you see, but you'll need to be up by 6:00, and the goats apparently don't take to strangers.'

'I think we'll take your word for it,' said mum with a smile, to which dad added a confirmatory nod.

'What happens to the milk?' asked dad.

'Someone else deals with it, though if you have porridge in the morning you'll get it there, and it gets made into soap. Julia, the middle daughter, named by Elise after Pieter's first wife who died of cancer soon after they had married, helps her mum. They'll be home from school by now, so we should get back and see them.'

Mum and dad were astonished that I ate "normal" food as we sat at an extremely noisy dining table that evening. It was Salmon en croute and I enjoyed every mouthful, though I had already confessed that on the previous day I had popped into the butcher's shop and bought myself a fresh sausage roll!

On the next day Elise drove us up the dale to visit, first, Askrigg, the village they recalled from the original tv programmes of *All Creatures Great and Small,* and then on to Hawes, where we had some lunch, and where even there some of the locals knew Elise and waved or said hello.

The next day, Friday was Market Day and mum was in her element, though dad was less enamoured and quickly found an excuse to pop into *The Golden Lion* as soon as it opened for a pint and whisky chaser. Meanwhile Elise had veg and fruit shopping to do for Fiene, who was less able to get about given that she was almost 80.

I did wonder how they would handle the ceremony of the Friday meal, presided over this time by Gale, but they said later how moved they were and honoured to share it with a rabbi and her three Jewish daughters.

'Are you still a rabbi?' asked dad as we ate and chatted.

'It's not as ordination is in the Catholic Church, whereby it claims some indelible ontological change, but it means that I am an authorised Jewish teacher, and I will remain that for the rest of my life.'

'But Lizzie tells me you are also a Catholic and isn't baptism meant to be for life?'

Elise smiled.

'I am simply Elise, and to my mother here, my husband Pieter, and my three daughters Grace, Julia and Gale, to Lizzie who is now with us, and I hope to you, that is who I am always.'

Dad had no idea how to respond.

'And believe me, that is quite enough,' said Pieter, gently

releasing the tension.

'Please believe me, Elise, I wasn't probing in any way, just interested,' said Dad

'You need never apologise, Ken. My life has contained some odd things, but when I look around the table, I can feel only great joy as to how it has worked out so far.'

'So far?' asked mum.

'Of course,' said Elise. 'It's always "so far" for we don't know what tomorrow might bring.'

'That's an important insight my Buddhism maintains,' I added. 'There is only now and it's in the present that we live.'

'I like the present,' said Gale, 'in every way and I think we should all be glad to be in it.'

I had noticed in my first week that, although Julia looked most like Elise, Gale was the most akin to Elise and often uttered words of wisdom spontaneously.

Saturday morning was hard as mum and dad packed the car and prepared to head north again, but I also knew it marked the end of my holiday, and that whatever lay before me I would now have to live.

A Picnic

On that same Saturday morning, after mum and dad had left, Elise suggested she and I go out for a walk and take a picnic up to the Middleham gallops where the local racing stable exercised their horses but apparently (and happily) not on a Saturday as they were all attending race meetings. I was glad to accept, and I imagine Elise must have realised that I would miss mum and dad so that a complete change would be therapeutic. She was quite right, for up there I could see Pen Hill and beyond up Wensleydale. The day was still and not too cold but we both had wrapped up well.

Elise carried the picnic basket prepared by Fiene and I carried the blanket we would use to sit on.

'This is my regular Shabbat retreat,' Elise said as we spread the blanket and brought out the food and the drink.

'How much do you still think of yourself as Jewish?' I asked.

'All the time – because being Jewish is not a religion, it is something I am, just as Aishe has brown skin. In terms of the practices Judaism regards as important I retain a mental picture rather than doing them. The idea of a special day for family life and doing as little as possible would be wholesome for everyone which is why I'm sorry Sunday is now mostly regarded as just another day, even though as a Jew Shabbat is the last day of the week, Saturday.

'Although I knew I had to leave behind all that had become part of Judaism over history, when I went to live as a solitary, nevertheless I was still a rabbi and proud to be but in a very different sort of way to how, say, a Catholic priest might think of himself. A rabbi is simply someone sufficiently trained to be authorised to act within a community in certain ways, primarily in terms of teaching and preaching. I'm certain that most Jews would think I was a bad rabbi in terms of practice of Judaism but there are tenets of that practice I hold to.

'Being one with my people constantly reminds me that 6 million of my people were murdered not so long ago, although that merely continued a pattern that lasted for 2000 years in different places mostly by Christian persecution. It is a reality that people hate Jews and I think they always will and find new reasons for doing so.

'As you know, I don't engage in beliefs, so my practice following on from my five years has taken two forms. The first is living with and loving my family, among whom I now include you, and this, I hope, extends out to loving others too, what Buddhism calls *Karuṇā* – Compassion. The second is *Shekinah*, the Presence. And I guess that whereas most people would approve of the former, about the latter they would be much more dismissive and possibly claim that I was talking nonsense. I don't care.

'I first became aware of *Shekinah* that terrible last night living alone, when the confirmation that the person I was talking to on the phone had succeeded in committing suicide whilst talking with me. For the first time in five years, I felt utterly lonely. I now understand that it was the experience of the absence of the Presence that had been with me throughout. The Carmelite Saints described this as desolation, though mercifully it lasted only until the following morning when I met Pieter, and the rest you know.'

'And to put it into terms a simple Buddhist might understand, how do you live with *Shekinah*? Do you do anything?'

'I want to share everything with you, Lizzie,' she said, pausing to eat. 'Unless Pieter has been called out in the night, I try to begin each day by making love.'

'What? Every day?' I answered, somewhat stunned.

Elise laughed.

'There are many ways of making love. You and I made love as we left the family and their dead baby, by the sheer intimacy of what we knew we had shared. No sexual act could compare with that and I'm far from sure Pieter would necessarily welcome my attention each morning before his work! But we cuddle and laugh and never cease to marvel at all that we have received in our life together. It may be just five minutes, but it matters, as it might be the only five minutes of the day when we can be together alone.

'By 5:30 I strive to be in my room, to light the candle and spend 30 minutes simply being in the Presence, or as you might put it, being in the present moment. After that it's goats and children, and whilst we still have her with us, I like to spend time drinking coffee and chatting with my beloved mother Fiene. There is often shopping to be done, and all the tasks that make up my day as daughter, wife and mother. What I mean is not that *Shekinah* dwells in my study as a catholic believes Christ is really present in the Sacrament in a special place called a tabernacle in the church, because the Presence is with me always, though I always seek to spend more time each day, perhaps a further hour and sometimes more, when I am, as the 46th psalm commands, to be still and know.'

'What you describe is so close to what Buddhism aims for, not a matter of doing things as such, but just being, though of course in itself that is perhaps the work of a lifetime for most people.'

'Yes, Lizzie, but it's not like that for you, is it? Which is why you felt able and perhaps compelled to leave Samye Ling to come here. I'm not suggesting you have achieved enlightenment because perhaps that is not possible, but I instinctively knew when we first spoke and I learned about your solitary retreat of three years and three months and three days, that we were what I dare to call soul-sisters, even though, ironically, we both would not even dare to suggest we have the first idea what a soul might be.'

'I regret to say,' I said, 'that I have read so very little non-Buddhist writings by or about those called mystics, which I know you have great familiarity with. But if I have understood the little I have read, might I dare suggest you are one with them, that they experience a direct union with what in various ways they might speak of the divine?'

'I am glad we are sitting on solid ground up here with a wonderful view around us of the beauty of the natural world, because that of which we are speak is considerably less than solid ground. It is fraught with potential pitfalls or, changing metaphors, we are skating on thin ice.

'It is true that some of those speaking of mystics use the sort of "union" language you refer to. And there are of course those who call themselves pantheists, amongst them the great Spinoza who speaks of everything being divine, or even panentheists who say we are within the divine, though both ideas, and they are only ideas, leave me cold. Neither take the Shoah seriously, let alone the many other experiences of pain, tragedy and death I have known.

'I do not, and as a Jew could never, speak of union with the divine. *Shekinah* is not that. Nor would I ever claim any sort of mystical experience because I find the language just too much and in a real sense simply ridiculous. We give names to everything to feel they are under our control. Aquinas wrote huge works defining the attributes of the deity and theologians of every religious tradition have done likewise. He, at least, at the end of his life decided his whole lifework was simply straw, but few others have been so modest. Religious people always claim too much.'

'I know you do not and never use the G word.'

'It is not because it is too holy to name as my fellow Jews claim, but because it is a word wholly devoid of any correlation with what cannot be named. The gods of history, the gods of popular belief, the gods of bad language, have no existence. You and I can climb Mount Olympus but we will not find Zeus, and that goes for all the other metaphorical mountains onto which human desperation places their fantasies. I sometimes uses the Hebrew *HaShem*, if I absolutely must, even though in practice that too has assumed the attribute of an actual name, instead of just meaning "The Name".'

'You're a hard taskmaster, Elise,' I said smiling. 'Not everyone has your experience nor capacity to express themselves as you can. What about we lesser mortals? Most people are terrified of silence.'

Elise laughed.

'I know that from every coffee shop I have ever entered which insist on constant background pop music, but I recognise what you are saying. The irony or paradox is that it is because I have hardly ever spoken about my experiences to Pieter and Fiene that they say they accept them precisely because I said so little or explained what I cannot. What worries me about religious groups is that they assume reticence or ambivalence show insincerity or lack of conviction when the opposite is the case. What most worries me is any conviction being shouted, it is as if the louder they shout, and I don't just mean volume, the more likely they are to be believed and thereby lead people astray into the deeper realms of nonsense.'

'But what can be done to stop that?' I asked.

'St Teresa of Avila looked upon contemplatives, as we might call them, as beacons or lighthouses in the darkness. I suspect she might say, as my own Jean-Pierre did, that we should just get on with the ordinariness of our living whilst holding fast to our discipline. That's not wildly exciting, and perhaps you might think that at least at Samye Ling you were able to influence the many who come.'

'Is a concern with Truth, spelt with a capital T, meant to be exciting?' I asked. 'Or even easily communicable to those coming on courses with other issues in mind?'

'I think, Lizzie, you have answered your own questions.'

'So,' and I paused, 'what is to be done, if anything? I've been on holiday and come back to find everything changed?'

We had finished our picnic and begun putting the bits and pieces together.

'I think the answer is that you and I can begin perhaps to find a way to best enable your practice to continue. My room is always there for you though at school-leaving time it can be quite noisy. I would be happy to share silence with you within the boundaries of what is possible, but we can set the room aside just for you at times that would be most helpful. It is so important to maintain your Buddhist practice which after all brought you here, even if you are happy to shed such aspects of it as you know best.'

'You are always so generous, Elise, but there is also the matter of how I engage in work. That is also part of practice. And I can't go on living with you.'

'Why not? Aren't you comfortable?'

'Oh yes, I'm loving being here but it's not fair on you all having me with you?'

'Nobody's complained, but a thought has just occurred to me. How would you feel about working part-time in the surgery? The afternoon receptionist is having to leave suddenly as her soldier husband is being moved from Catterick to Larkhill on Salisbury Plain. Pieter only found this out yesterday. It's a job requiring a love of animals and even some of the owners!'

I laughed.

'The morning receptionist, Meredith, deals with matters to do with staff and finance. In the afternoon it's about answering the phone, welcoming owners, and dealing with payments. Sometimes it's about counselling. I think you'd be good at it. You'd be paid of course, but as for continuing to live with us, I very much hope you will do so because, other than Leah and soon perhaps Aishe, you are the only person I can speak to about what we both know. We all like you very much. At least until you cannot bear us any longer, I would wish you to stay.'

'Of course I will stay, and perhaps I can talk to Pieter about the job later.'

'I love picnics in the open air up here. They're so useful for getting our minds sorted,' said Elise.

Neither Orgy nor Arguments

What would happen now I wondered, as we came down not exactly from the mountain, but from the Gallops above the Ure Valley? In a strange way as we walked back to the car and drove down to our home without any words between us, I felt for a brief moment as I had when brought face to face with Kanchenjunga the holy Mountain I had visited in my last weeks in Nepal.

As she parked the car, speaking for the first time since we had concluded our picnic, I told this to Elise. She grinned.

'When Moses came down from the mountain he was met with an explosion of erotic madness, and in the New Testament after what is known as the Transfiguration, Yeshua and his 3 disciples descended to be met with the other followers fighting among themselves about which of them was the most important. So, prepare yourself for when we walk in through the door. Who knows what we shall find.'

In fact, all was quiet within. The girls were visiting their friends, Fiene was having a rest on her bed, and Pieter was fast asleep on the sofa watching sport on television. Elise looked at me and smiled.

'Neither orgy nor arguments,' she said. 'I'm sure you know your fellow Scot Edwin Muir's greatest poem "The Transfiguration":

"Was it a vision

Or did we see that day the unseeable
One glory of the everlasting word
Perpetually at work, though never seen
Since Eden locked the gate that's everywhere
And nowhere? Was the change in us alone,
And the enormous earth still left forlorn,
An exile or a prisoner? Yet the world
We saw that day made this unreal, for all
was in its place?"

'And that world, it seems, includes my beloved husband snoring on the sofa!'

I laughed and the noise woke Pieter.

'Oh hello, how was the picnic?' he said somewhat bleary-eyed.

'What time are you expecting the children back?'

'When their tummies tell them it's time for food. Fish and chips night they won't miss.'

I returned to my own room and found that Fiene had already changed the linen and no doubt had already put mum and dad's into the wash. I had missed my wonderfully soft bed during their stay and lay down upon it for just a few moments. Almost two hours later (!) there was a knock on the door that woke me up. It was Elise asking my fish and chip requirements.

After tea my mum phoned to say they were safely home, and to tell me that a letter had come from Samye Ling which I asked her to open and read it to me.

'It's from Rinpoche and says that clearly you need a slightly longer break than you had agreed with him, so he was happy for you to stay another few days but asks that you let him know the date of your return.'

'Thanks mum. I will write tomorrow and post it Monday saying definitively that I am not returning. Should I mention the issue of all the money I brought with me when I became a nun.'

'All I think you need to say, and I've talked this over with dad, is that assuming your departure is permanent, say that your dad will be making contact to sort out the matter of your personal effects and finance. I think it best you leave this to us. I also want to say how happy I have been to see you there with Elise and her family.'

'You do know that being here is not a lessening of my commitment to meditation, but tomorrow I shall be exploring with Pieter the possibility of part-time work at the surgery.'

'That would be wonderful, my darling.'

'Mum, I want to thank you and dad so much for never saying anything even slightly like "I told you so" when I have made major changes in my life. Your constant love has meant so much and means even more now.'

On the following morning, I waited until I heard Elise go out to milk the goats, and then went into her room where the candle of *Shekinah* was burning bright. I sat down, adopted my full lotus position and felt wholly at ease as I entered meditation once again after some quietly sung Tibetan prayers. Elise had told me to close the door completely as everyone knew it meant no disturbance. Automatically at the end of the hour, my body knew it was time to end. I looked again at the candle and was powerfully aware that I had not been alone in that past hour.

I found Fiene and Elise chatting in the kitchen when I entered, and I was immediately welcomed with a bowl of porridge. It was never the off-white colour I had been used to before coming here but was slightly brown, containing as it did flax and other tiny seeds which were meant to be helpful for digestion. All that mattered was that it tasted good.

'It is,' said Elise, 'the first day of the week – Sunday. We keep the Jewish calendar here, except of course we don't. The girls won't be up early, that's for certain, though it's now half-term so early mornings will be quiet. I gave Julia the morning off dairy duty but she has said that during half-term she is hoping I can begin teaching her how to milk and care for the goats. Pieter is outside the yard washing the car and Land Rover. I mentioned to him the idea that you might consider the job of afternoon receptionist and he welcomed the idea and says you will need to meet Heidi and Fran, the two vets with whom you will be working, plus the nurses. But we agreed there would no problem and he's happy for you to have a chat with him and go into the surgery this morning and see the set-up.'

'What do Heidi and Fran specialise in?'

'They both have families and so work part-time dealing almost exclusively with small animals. Fran is Czech and so, like you, struggles to speak English, but Heidi comes from here.'

'You're very rude.'

'Don't worry, Lizzie,' said Fiene who was loading the dishwasher, 'my lovely daughter struggles to speak any recognisable form of Dutch when we visit the Netherlands, and your accent is much easier for me, even after all this time, than the majority of locals.'

I went out to the car park where Pieter seemed to be getting as wet as the two vehicles he was meant to be washing. To my great relief he turned the hose off as I approached. He led me into the surgery and showed me round.

'It would be great if you could do this, Lizzie,' he said, 'not because I want to exploit you, but it will be very handy if anything comes in at the weekend as well of course in the afternoon. Everything needs to be computerised and you might be able to do it whilst I'm out on a farm.'

'I'd be happy to learn. I imagine I need to get the ok from Fran and Heidi and receive the once over by the nurses.'

'Oh no. It's my practice and I make the final decisions but come in on Monday and meet the team that from then on you will be part of.'

There was, however, one question I wanted to ask Pieter as we sat down in the surgery on that Sunday.

'As you know, Pieter, Elise and I have both had long periods of living alone in total silence, very long indeed by most standards. Knowing even a little of what this means for Elise in her daily living, how does this affect you?'

'It's never intruded into our life, if that's what you mean, in terms of being husband and wife or parents, and certainly not in the sort of ways in which mine does. She doesn't get up in the middle of the night to attend a calving for example, and although she does sometimes come in from the goats a bit smelly, I can outdo that most days.

'What has always amazed me about her ever since we met is her lack of necessity in talking about what is closest to the centre of her life. A lot, or most, religious people need to tell you about it as if to justify what they think and do, but Elise is so at ease with it all. I'm not even sure what I mean by that, but it's such a natural part of her life and therefore our life as a family. When I first met her, it was that ease and confidence about what she knew and never needed to speak of, that convinced me that what I didn't know I could accept.'

'Yes, you're quite right about religious obsession and its apparent need to justify it by telling others. Actually, though it's not a very politically correct thing to say, that is very much the same dynamic in gay men and women, the need to talk about it almost as if by talking about it in the hope of winning acceptance they can convince themselves.'

'You had lots of religious people coming to the monastery I gather, visitors and the curious. Did you find that there?'

'Oh constantly. It drove me mad. One of the good things about being here with you is that nobody asks me about it. Elise knows and that really matters to me because it makes me feel no longer lonely, but even she and I don't discuss theory very much even though sometimes I want to ask her something.'

'I think you've just said something so important, Lizzie. We have a wonderful family life with mama and the children, but I think that special part of Elise's life was a cause of loneliness too. Having someone with whom to share, and it's because you too have undergone the solitary refinement as she calls it, I already sense since you've been here a new ease in her, almost a release of reserved energy. As a vet I mostly only deal with bodies of various sorts, and I'm far from sure that I'm using the right words but it's as if she can breathe more easily, now she has a soul-sister.'

'I feel the same, Pieter, even though our points of departure have been quite different, there has been a convergence.'

On later reflection I found my conversation with Pieter had enabled both of us to articulate something very important about which it was never easy to speak. He was a lovely man, so very good-looking in his 50s, and a man who had known the great pain of the loss of his first wife Julia, many years before. And in so many ways, he reflected something of the same wisdom I always found in his mother Fiene. She was now almost 80 and still very active in the home, cooking and constantly aware of the needs of the family, not least the 3 girls who loved being with her. I counted myself to be so very lucky to be here, or put better, glad to have been brought here by the circumstances of *Karuṇā*.

But from Monday, there I was a receptionist in a veterinary surgery handling a computer (with help from Meredith), being nice to a miscellany of creatures, but above all above all being with and reassuring people. It was they who really needed my attention because people get so attached to their animals that anything happening to them causes anxieties. Fortunately, the practice was blessed with two gentle women vets, Fran and Heidi and nurses. Both women worked half-time and so I was mostly working alongside Heidi except when they were involved in major surgical procedures when they worked closely together.

A couple of months into settling into my new life, I learned from Elise that through various events in the town she had come into contact with the leaders of the church community, amongst them the diocesan bishop. Out of the blue one day came a phone call from the Bishop asking Elise if she might be willing to come to his diocesan conference of all the clergy which was to be held at the Butlins holiday camp in Skegness. He wanted her to come and speak about silence in her life and the place it might have in Christian prayer. She was hesitant and said she would call back and let him know.

'I'm really surprised,' she said as she told me about the invitation. 'Our previous contacts seemed to leave him extremely uncomfortable, and I assumed I would have no further contact, but what do you think? If I was to do it, I would want you there too and I would make it clear that we are a double-act.'

'I would certainly be very happy to go with you, to drive you there and back and so on, but it's you he wants to speak and perhaps you can do so without betraying the profound restraint we both experience when it comes to saying anything to anyone.'

'If we do go, I wonder whether I might persuade Aishe to come with us too. She comes from a third tradition and under your own guidance is growing into silence. I know that, because she tells me what a good teacher of meditation you are. If there are questions about mindfulness you might be on hand to clarify the differences I know you feel between mindfulness and Buddhism. Let's do it, sister,' she said with conviction. And so, once she said yes, the three of us headed to Skeggie, as it is known, for a night in a chalet being looked after by redcoats!

Butlins at Skeggie

'Sisters and brothers,' said the diocesan bishop, 'it gives me great pleasure to introduce to you Rabbi Elise Westernberg, though if by the end of her words this morning she leaves you feeling any more comfortable than she did when I first met her, I shall be surprised.'

Elise smiled.

'Elise trained as a rabbi in London and Jerusalem, speaks Hebrew, ancient and modern, Arabic and "gets by" (her words) in Greek and Latin, a rare-female Talmud scholar which she taught to students for the rabbinate. She now lives in the Yorkshire Dales where, she has a herd of goats which she milks each day, is married to a Dutch vet, and have three daughters still at school. Please give a warm welcome to Rabbi Elise.'

The clergy gathered for their tri-annual conference (leaving behind, as was joked by the bishop, a skeleton staff to deal with funerals!), did as they were asked.

'Thank you', began Elise. 'Though I have lived in this country for over 30 years and in Yorkshire for the majority of that time, you may still hear the occasional hint of my native Canadian corruption of the English language in much the same way as modern church services manage to corrupt the pure English of the Book of Common Prayer!'

There was laughter.

'I want to begin by giving you an account of something that happened just last year. A friend had just received an unwelcome diagnosis from a consultant and as she emerged, she felt she needed to sit and be quiet to take it in. Adjacent to the doctor's offices was a church with open doors and she went in. It turned out that on this weekday afternoon there was about to be the service of Evensong which was to be led by a woman priest. As she sat down on a pew designed not even slightly for comfort, my friend was greeted with just five words: "Have you got a smartphone?"'

There was some nervous laughter.

'My friend had no idea what she was talking about, and the priest explained that they used an app with which to pray. My friend smiled and left. I shall therefore risk offending some of you by saying that just as pornography on a phone is not sexual love, neither is using an app, prayer.'

There was a sense of unease.

'I didn't know I was Jewish until I was 20. My parents were anti-religious in a big way and had never told me that my mother was Jewish, as was her mother, and that my great grandparents had died in the Shoah, the Holocaust. Judaism is passed only through the female line. To be a Jew means you have a Jewish mother regardless of who your father is.

'I didn't know until after I became a rabbi, and this might blow your minds as much as it did mine, that I am also a Roman Catholic, having been baptised and confirmed when just three days old in my hometown in Canada. My full name therefore is Elise Mary Westernberg, Mary being of course the English translation of the original Hebrew name of Miriam and my surname is Dutch. My husband is a direct descendent of the Renaissance artist family of Breughel, though to be honest he failed miserably to paint the bedroom when I asked.

There was a release of tension as people laughed.

'It was on a visit back to see my dying aunt in Canada that I met the priest who had baptised me all those years earlier. Until that day, I hadn't even known of his existence, so I was amazed when he began by saying he had been waiting for me to return, and he told me about my Catholic baptism and confirmation. In old age, he was now living as a hermit in a Canadian forest and as a result of the short time we spent together in his hermitage, when I returned to the UK after my aunt's death, I resigned from my work as a rabbi, bought a small building abandoned by the RAF on the North York Moors, close to the sea, and for five years lived as a Solitary. My only outside contacts were the farmer (a man of few words, trust me!) who taught me how to milk cows which I did each morning, an occasional greeting to the postman or on my monthly encounter with the person who brought my food from the supermarket in Scarborough.

'Each day I spent four hours in what might be called an even greater silence than that in which I was living, in what I called my *Waiting Room*. I engaged in no religious practice, Jewish or Christian, nor any other tradition, but for two hours each morning and two hours towards evening I sat in silence, simply waiting.

'It took me three years of silence in the Waiting Room finally to clear my head of all the religious and philosophical junk I had brought with me. In the last two years I managed at last to be ready for whatever it was I was waiting for, however long it would take to come, as the priest who had baptised me had to wait almost 30 years for me to arrive at his door in the forest. He knew it would happen, and in my own setting so did I.

'It will already be clear to some of you, perhaps all, that I am not a theist in the sense that theism had dominated western thinking in Judaism, Christianity and Islam for the past 3,000 years, referring to a divine being operating as a kind of cosmic engineer, who is sometimes, albeit wholly unreliably, on call. I eschew labels, but I might at least for the purposes of my being here with you, say I'm a non-theist, by which I mean that by discovery over five years living completely alone waiting, the language and thought forms of theism make no sense, akin to speaking of colour to the blind, or music to those without hearing.

'Hebrew scholars among you might know the word שְׁכִינָה (transliterated as *Shekinah*). It comes from the Talmud, not the Bible, and means the dwelling or Presence with a capital P. It's not just because I'm a Jew that I do not use the G word, but primarily because it has become, first by overuse and then by abuse, utterly and completely devoid of meaning in our world today. How odd it is that the G word and that of the Jew whose name was Yeshua, whom you worship, are with the F-word, the commonest swear words in the English language.

'As an aside, may a Jew ask whether it is anti-Semitic for Christians to avoid using יְהוֹשֻׁעַ, Yehoshua or Yeshua, in favour of the Greek translation made by Paul? You all know what he was actually called, so why not use that? Paul was deliberately trying to be what we would now call anti-Semitic in concealing the actual origins of his new religion, and even going so far as to change his own name. So why does this continue? But that is an aside.

'I also do not use the G word because it means or implies to many, including people such as Richard Dawkins, the form of theism he very effectively rejects. It is little more than an updated version of the deities that have been believed in from earliest times – someone up there or wherever, apparently personal, to whom we talk, using the deity as a form of Transitional Object, a grown-up form of the teddies children have and talk to. And the language of that religion continued to develop in terms drawn from the world of human hierarchy, at the top of which there is one addressed as Lord, King, Almighty, Worshipful and many more in Judaism, Christianity and Islam, as if we are addressing a potentate of some kind but simply reflecting the world views of those living at the times such things were first spoken. Even the word "Father" is for many women and some men, a mental link to unpleasant or worse experiences of a male parent.

'Some of you will find this challenging, but our mindset shapes our prayer. When my husband shouts at the television watching his beloved Holland play football, I tell him "They can't hear you", but I was struck by his reply, "I know, but it makes me feel better". That has enabled me to see the value of spoken and most forms of mental prayer as essentially what it does to us, not that we might just be twisting the hands of a potentate or as we might call on a computer expert when something goes wrong. It is akin to the talking therapy of which we know that by just giving expression to feeling can change within, but changes nothing without, unless we ourselves decide to act on it.

'I suspect I might be deluged by claims of prayers that have worked, that the unlooked for has happened, but the unexpected does happen more often than we might imagine, as any doctor, or even a vet, will tell you, and isolated claims make for a bad rule. A celestial engineer providing the things we are desperately hoping for in one case or another but did nothing to prevent the murder of my great grandparents and 6 million of my other fellow Jews and others in the camps, plus all the horrendous suffering across human history who prayed no less earnestly than you or I might. I think also of the many in church services when the Lisbon earthquake struck on All Saints Day, 1755, or the Boxing Day 2004 tsunami claiming 230,000 lives in a matter of moments, not a few of whom died in their churches in Sri Lanka on a Sunday morning.

'I care little for beliefs, as most religious beliefs are of the type described in *Alice Through The Looking Glass*, as six impossible things believed in before breakfast. What someone tells me they believe, tells me nothing about the content of the belief, whether it is true or not, but always a great deal about the believer.

'A belief is an epiphenomenon of the brain caused by many

factors. To the best of my extremely limited knowledge, you here place a statement of belief at the heart of all your Sunday services, which I would hazard the suggestion is extremely brave of you, but I can well imagine that if any of you were to ask members of your church what their religious beliefs were, few would respond with either of the creeds of Nicea. But of course, even without a formal creed, Jewish services embody beliefs in prayers, though as with all religious folk I have met, their personal religion does not often match the official version.

'I will risk saying this because I know that Christians, or at least some, will disagree, but to imagine that by simply saying "I believe in x, y or z", you now stand on the other side of the Jordan River, seems to me absurd. When I realised that I was Jewish, I set about discovering what the beliefs of a Jew were in order to belong. Only very slowly and, even before living as a solitary, did I come to realise that beliefs are little more than the reflection of propositions generated by and then passed on from previous generations which must be tested in the light of daily circumstances which is the only place when and where we encounter the ultimate Reality of שְׁכִינָה.

'In entering into the Waiting Room, not even knowing for how long I might be there, I knew instinctively that I had to lay down beliefs, opinions and even religious language itself, and that I had to take other things with me, above all my personal experiences in which I had witnessed suffering and death, especially the deaths of children at which I had been present. And because I am a Jew, I never lost sight of the terrible histories of my ethnic identity, often regrettably at the hands of Christians, heavily influenced by the hateful and shameful anti-Semitic writings of Martin Luther on the German mindset culminating in the Shoah, the man you still commemorate in your Anglican liturgical calendar, and as a Jew I feel deeply disturbed that you do so. Whatever else I was waiting for had to accept the suffering I was bringing. There are no slick answers to the suffering of children born severely brain-damaged or with cancer, and unless what I encountered could enter into the pains and suffering, without glib response, then I knew that was not what I was waiting for.

The arrival came unexpectedly through another intimate involvement with suffering and suicide, and that was when I knew it was ok to live with שְׁכִינָה and that my time in silence could end safely. On the very next morning I met and fell in love with the vet who was doing the TB testing of the cows I had been milking earlier.

'But I haven't been invited here to criticise what you do or how you think, and I assume that in the main you are good people, and one or two, no doubt very good, though I must add at once something so very important that I have learned. My experience of שְׁכִינָה, lived daily, has *not* made me a better person, and from observation, Christians do not necessarily behave better than others, and sometimes worse, but that's not the point. Replacing the reality of שְׁכִינָה with which I live with morality would seem to me be a loss not a gain, even when the world seems wholly unconcerned with even the possibility of Truth.

'Around us in the west, some traditional forms of religion are in decline and open expressions of atheism increasing. Falling numbers mean an increase of those who, in the words of Lewis Carroll, must run faster and faster to remain standing where they are. I have been told that more and more clergy across the whole Church, but especially in rural areas, are having to serve larger and larger numbers of parishes and I feel so sorry for you as I imagine that more of your time must be spent managing diminishing resources.

'How then should this crisis be faced? You will all have your own thoughts about this, but I have an abiding concern for all those who find themselves having to do not what they thought had originally brought them to ordination.

'So, be guided by Tony Benn! He said that he was leaving parliament to give more time to politics. I gave up the rabbinate to give myself body and soul to שְׁכִינָה. Might it just be that you should all, even bishops and those bizarrely named creatures "archdeacons", and I cannot for the life of me imagine what they are, stop running around like the religious form of headless chickens. The world will not be saved by more, better managed, religion, but by men and women living as St Teresa of Avila said, as beacons in the gathering dark.

'You are in "holy orders" and I can't tell you how to use your time because you will know better than me about fund-raising and something called Parochial Church Councils (and someone afterwards might tell me whether "parochial" is a noun or an adjective, because the difference would be considerable!) but I cannot think what your holiness can consist of if it amounts to spending less than at least one hour each day, perhaps in two parts, in silence waiting upon the Source and Origin of all things.

'Even as you do so, however, you will find it hard, even the saints among you. If you don't believe me, read St John of the Cross and countless others who have felt that it is only in waiting upon the divine in a disciplined way, and especially when you find silence bores and scares you, that what is called prayer might lead us deeper into the heart of all things. Because if we're not doing that, because if we're too busy raising funds and doing a thousand and one other things, including the endless pursuit of the latest gimmicks or even supposedly praying with the latest gadgets, then you have admitted defeat and in contrast to Tony Benn, you have chosen to give up what is most important. Just what then have you to offer those you are called to serve?

'If this can be your way forward, you will at times, and perhaps more than just at times, come to hate silence, I would then urge you to hold fast in the silence to the very things that to many contradict all we are about, by which I mean the intensities of suffering you all will have encountered in your work. If you can do that and continue, I can only assure you that my own experience has not been to discover answers to make us feel somehow excused when we are bidden to give a reply, but the awareness of שְׁכִינָה.

'Those of you who have visited Jerusalem will, I hope, have included time spent at יָד וַשֵׁם (*Yad Vashem*, literally "a memorial and a name") the memorial to those murdered by the Nazis. If so, you will know what I mean by the silence which can be the only response to what you see and hear there. Religions of whatever sort maintaining this has nothing to do with the truths they proclaim or offer a religion of escape from the realities either in forms of quietism such as mindfulness, or in the multiplicity of words are of course free to think whatever they want, but thinking does not make it so.

'I will end by quoting a Greek Orthodox monk of Mt Athos, now canonised as St Silouan the Athonite. In the silence of my five years in the Waiting Room I sought never to go beyond his words: "Keep your mind in hell, and despair not". This is for what you and I were ordained.'

Elise sat down to silence before the gathered assembly gave her applause.

The bishop rose to offer thanks.'

'Sisters and brothers, you can't say I didn't warn you, and I hope that in your groups you might find some questions for Elise to consider, though I know that quite often she recognises the questions as more real than any possible answers might be. She is here with two close colleagues, Sonā, who is a Buddhist nun, who herself lived in solitary silence for over three years and teaches meditation, and Aishe, who works as a speech therapist but is rooted in meditation in the Hindu tradition. They will be around until lunchtime tomorrow and would be more than willing to share their experiences with you.

'But Elise, thank you for the courage and honesty with which you have spoken to us. Those were the qualities I knew you would bring, together with your constant awareness of *Shekinah*.'

There was further applause.

Response

Elise needed to have a period of rest after her talk and therefore did not join everyone for lunch. Aishe and I decided to split up and see what sort of response Elise's address had made. We had already decided that we would only speak about what we knew, so questions about church organisation we consistently replied with "I don't know and so obviously cannot say".

The various conversations we had, and Elise herself was around in the afternoon, seemed to be divided between those who genuinely wanted to know more about how to manage silence when it genuinely left them feeling uncomfortable, those who wished to understand how it might relate to what they called the beliefs of the church, and those who were unquestionably hostile, and I think it would be fair to say that most of these came from the so-called evangelical wing of the church who, it seemed to me, did not have beliefs but certainties. Some even said that silence let in the devil and condemned all other religions as the work of Satan. At all times we were determined to be polite.

The clergy met in their groups in the evening to draw up some questions for Elise and me on the following morning, Aishe feeling she did not have either the experience or the knowledge to answer any that might come theologically loaded. I had long since been used to answering a torrent of questions at Samye Ling.

The first was "Is what you have said Biblical?", to which Elise's immediate response was to say 'Surely what matters is whether or not it is true? You might question any aspect of life today asking whether it is Biblical. Our system of government, democracy, for example is nowhere taught in the Bible as determinative. In-vitro fertilisation is not even hinted at in the Bible and other aspects of our life which have brought great joy to so many. Though I have obviously not looked thoroughly enough, I have found no mention of Archdeacons or other titles beloved of the clergy, and I could say much more.

'As a former teacher of Tanakh, what you call the Old Testament, and a thorough knowledge of your own New Testament, a work mostly concerned with a Jewish man however bowdlerised by another Jewish man called Saul, I would imagine that even in your diocese it would be quite impossible to find any sort of agreement about the authority of scripture that would satisfy you all. And that is important, because most of the things we fight for and insist upon are simply beliefs, not self-evidently true.'

A man in the audience called out. 'I know my prayers are answered and I've witnessed wonderful things.'

Elise smiled.

'Ok' she replied. 'Seeing wonderful things is great, though one of the reasons I had five years wrestling with the angel, as did Jacob at the brook Jabbok, is that I had seen at first hand terrible things, and I'm reminded of a story about James Joyce, who was asked at Geneva Airport by an American fan if he could shake the hand that wrote Ulysses. Joyce replied "I shouldn't if I were you because it's done a lot of other things besides"'

There was a lot of laughter.

'And am I reminded of this because when my husband comes in and takes hold of my hand, I sometimes find myself thinking of where his hand has been that day, because he is a large animal vet. But times without number he has reported than an animal he thought would not make the previous night had made a huge improvement for no obvious or apparent reason. No one prayed for this cow, sheep or pig and it just happened. I would urge you to say no more than that you *believe* these prayers have been answered. They are proof of nothing and will be held reprehensible and silly by those who prayed no less intently and experienced no such wonderful things. You are in danger of making *HaShem* a lottery.'

There was some applause.

The second question was about mindfulness and how many people found it helpful, so why was Elise critical of it? She turned to me.

'It is undoubtedly helpful for a lot of people,' I began, 'and is usually well-marketed as being of assistance to their well-being and functioning. There is nothing wrong in that and in fact I'm sure it is to be welcomed. However, Elise knows from our conversations that I am sceptical about it for two reasons. The first is that it offers techniques, some of which are drawn from Buddhism, to enhance the consumer society. Mindfulness will enhance your performance and so on, but it separates those techniques from the context in which they originated which came with built-in safety, and of which I fear many of those offering it know little or nothing.

'But the other difficulty I have as a Buddhist, follows on from something someone said to me last evening at the meal table. He said that all he had been taught at theological college was really worthless because it wasn't relevant to the actual concerns of people who never asked him about most of what he had been taught in his lectures and tutorials. Perhaps others of you will identify with that, but I would urge you not to water down the fundamentals to make it easy. Since when do the concerns about meaning and purpose in our lives have to be easy just to satisfy a world that wants everything packaged in bite-sized chunks. Am I or am I not about something I have asked myself as a Buddhist nun, something I have given years of my life not just to studying but to living? And I would ask it of you too. We all live with the subtle wiles of reductionism and that is why I can share wholly with Elise in urging silence, or silent prayer as you might call it, as the basis of this holding firm. That's why I am sceptical about mindfulness. It is just watered down Buddhism, and it wouldn't surprise me, though I don't know, that there are those within your own traditions who think that diluting is the way forward. Hear it from a Buddhist nun and Catholic Rabbi: it is not.'

Ironically, given that the main speaker at this event was Elise, this received a rapturous response and clearly spoke to many people.

Elise was now asked how much time as a busy wife and mother she was able to give to silence.

'This is a good question because my answer might perhaps help those of you who are also busy people with families. I rise at 5:30 in order to have a full 30 minutes silence before milking the goats and joining my daughters for their breakfast and seeing them off to school. After that there is usually shopping to be done and cleaning, but I normally spend at least a further hour before the girls come home from school. It is a matter of priorities and as I asked you yesterday, for what or for Whom (with a capital W) did you get ordained?

The next question for Elise was about religious syncretism and whether she was advocating some general religion made up of bits and pieces.

'Most definitely not. Soṇā is a Buddhist nun of the Tibetan

tradition, Aishe is learning more and more of her roots in Hinduism, and I am a Jewish Catholic. We never try to influence one another to change or adopt another tradition, but we love one another in our differences and seek to spend time in silence together as often as possible, Soṇā and I every day, because whatever we might want to think of what some call *HaShem*, we are not the sole possessors and what matters is what we share already. I will be honest and dare say to you clerics, that I do not like religion because essentially it's about claims to truth that effectively close us to others and aggrandise some at the expense of the many.'

I suspected that the bishops were now feeling that Elise was on dangerous ground as far as their authority was concerned and began to draw the session to a close. I sensed this especially in the degree of effusive thanks he provided suggesting that the sooner we left the better!

As we drove back after lunch, I asked Elise if she thought it had been worthwhile.

'Not at all, and it has reaffirmed my determination never to repeat anything like it. Whereof one cannot speak one must remain silent, and its corollary, there's none so deaf as those who do not wish to hear.'

'One or two people did raise with me the question of how to begin silent meditation,' said Aishe, 'but no one seemed able to understand the difference between what we know as silence and meditation *about* something or other, which is of course thinking by another name.'

'Yes,' I added, 'I had a number of those conversations too. And what struck me were those who turned defensiveness into aggression. I sincerely hope that at Samye Ling that was never done by members of the Sangha as they met with groups or individuals who disagreed with them. It seems to me a basic matter of good manners.'

'And yet, I can't help thinking,' said Elise to me, as we continued up the A1(M), 'that the greatest impact was made by you when you spoke this morning about the dangers of watering down and pandering to the worst aspect of modern society which demands everything be made simple and accessible. You got a great round of applause for that.'

'Although I'm happy to no longer wear my robes or shave my head and even eat meat now I live in the Dales and recognise that there is a lot of Buddhism which is simply a hangover from the culture dominant when these things came to be, I still want to hold fast to certain fundamentals that underlie my practice.'

'And does that include *Shekinah*?' asked Elise.

I said "certain" fundamentals, those to do with meditation, but not all. I do hold fast to *Shekinah* for two reasons. The first is that you have never sought to define it or impose it – you just get on with it as the central reality of your heart. The second is my own experience which I cannot deny. I don't yet have the same continuous awareness that you and Leah have, but enough to make me think that the pair of you are not just *schlemiels*.'

'Hey Aishe,' said Elise laughing from the back seat, 'the Buddhist is speaking Yiddish now, and says I'm not a fool, even though it feels almost like being damned with faint praise.'

By now all three of us were laughing as we approached the exit for Bedale and home beyond in the welcoming Dales.

'And,' I added further, 'there is a third reason for holding fast to *Shekinah* and it lies in our ability to laugh even about the most sacred.'

'Yes, you're quite right,' said Elise. 'Jews have given humour to the world and even dare to tease *HaShem*. That is a sign of wholeness.'

'I passed the bar on my way to bed last night,' said Aishe, 'and there was a lot of noise and a lot of drinking, and a great deal of loud laughter, but it didn't feel to me a sign of wholeness, rather the opposite, almost a sign of hopelessness.'

'It must be tough for so many of them,' said Elise, 'Either they are asked to take on impossible workloads or they struggle on endeavouring to fight against the dominant *weltanschauung* which not so much rejects what they have to offer but pays it no attention which is worse. At least people hate Jews which is certainly better than being simply ignored.'

'We can see that at home,' said Aishe. 'I heard someone say of the vicar that she was nice, but I don't see crowds flocking into her services, and that goes also for the Methodists, on the basis of being nice and generally inoffensive. I've never heard anyone say that of you, Elise.'

We all laughed.

'It's not our role to be public,' responded Elise. 'Perhaps things will get sufficiently worse, and our silent role will have a place, but as far as I'm concerned, today ends my public utterances. I hope we've given all those well-meaning clergy something to challenge and encourage them to think differently about what they are there for, but I don't come home optimistic about that.'

'I agree,' I said. 'I sat in at their service of Morning Prayer this morning. Some of them were using mobile phones or tablets to take part, but it was just words, words, words, with a token couple of minutes silence at the end, possibly in the hope of pleasing their Buddhist interloper.'

'You should have offered some of your Tibetan chant. I sometimes hear you singing it as you begin meditation first thing, and I find it deeply moving and take the feeling out with me to the goats.'

'Yes, I recall that from our visit to Samye Ling,' added Aishe. 'I sometimes listen to it on YouTube. It's not in any kind of western mode but running through it is a powerful sense of energy which feeds my meditation.'

'I would happily teach both of you some basic chants with which to annoy your husbands, if you wish,' I said, laughing.

'Don't worry,' replied Aishe, ' I already have lots of ways for doing that.'

Normal

There is little to say about normal life other than that it is what happens all the time and contains little that is special and out of the ordinary, and yet I have never minded things just going on much as they did the day before. Not that working in a veterinary surgery didn't produce moments of joy and dismay for owners and their small animals. When I began, I often shed tears when an animal had to be euthanised (I personally still prefer "put to sleep"), but as with everything you get used to even such events as more or less normal in work. The thing about normal life is that it goes by more quickly than we sometimes imagine day by day. Suddenly it's a new year or a birthday, and the older I get the faster these things seem to come round.

In the following months and years, I tried to keep my mind fed by Buddhist writing though increasingly I was drawing much closer to Elise's non-religious approach to meditation and silence. Not that she eschewed her Judaism, nor that of her daughters, and the weeks and years were punctuated by remembrance of Jewish life. This she continued to share with her oldest friend Leah who still practised a more explicit Judaism with her partner Ursula in their home village of Pateley Bridge. She always said that religions too easily got trapped into trying to tie things down for the sake of safety, whereas we were concerned in the end what is True, even if that could never be spoken of.

I did, after needing some encouragement from Elise, agree to teach two women who made contact all about Buddhism and meditation in the Buddhist tradition. Word of mouth meant that others also made contact. There was nowhere here for a gathering of even four people with me, though I did meet with and meditated with individuals in what I still thought of as Elise's room and where those who came in were immediately interested in the candle that continued to burn there. I said very little about that, but I did discover that a small room at the rugby club on the road to Hawes might be available except when used by burly gentlemen giving every appearance of engaging in lawful physical assault! I was able to offer a small number of half-day teaching and practice sessions in the summer months when it was not cold and in use.

Sometimes I spoke about my time in Nepal and occasionally wondered whether Jampa was still at Namobuddha Monastery or had returned to Australia as Brett. It was now a very long time ago and I wondered what he might think of how I had been living my Buddhism here in the Yorkshire. It would, I thought, be wonderful to return and see Hilepani and our dear Hanka and her family, and to drive north to the see the great goddess of the sky, Sagarmāthā, Everest. Even more I wished to see Kanchenjunga at least once more before I died. When I mentioned this to Fiona and Elise over porridge one morning, they both encouraged me to make plans and do this, and of course I knew I could well afford it, so I began to plan a trip to Nepal. It would be in the following January when tourists were fewer and the climate bearable. When I told Naomi of my plans, she said she was jealous. She had already been back with Andrea and hoped it would go well.

Another piece of news came in the form of a letter from Gemma, the mother of the dying baby whom Elise had baptised, to say that not only had she and Scott a new baby daughter, but that she had returned to her Christian origins and had just been accepted as a candidate for ordination in the Episcopal Church. Elise whooped with joy at the news.

'I think it shows that my baptism "took"!' she said, laughing.

'It was a small act of *Karuṇā*,' I said, 'but just consider what it has done for her and for me.'

'*Karuṇā* is surely always like that. I often read some of your Buddhist writings and find so very much in them that is genuinely helpful to my understanding of all sorts of things.'

'I didn't know that.'

'I don't go into your room, but sometimes you leave a book in here. What do you think of the "religionless" Buddhism of someone such as Stephen Batchelor? He was a Zen Buddhist, a Tibetan Buddhist and now lives happily married in central France, commuting to his fan club for retreats in England and America.'

'I understand what he is trying to do. He wants to distance meditation practice from its historical roots and all it acquired en route in the way of what he now thinks encumbrances. I suppose I have made a slightly similar journey. Just look at me and you can see for yourself: jumper and jeans and long hair, and I eat whatever the wonderful Fiene puts before us. But I also think that if he tries to cut the present off from the past, whatever he is doing will die with him. All religious traditions take root in the particular, not the abstract, and that is how they are passed down. Might I even suggest that is how you live out your own Judaism.'

'Yes, of course, though being Jewish is not a religious choice, it is what I am by birth as Aishe's skin is the colour it is because as with me it has been passed on over centuries. I sometimes worry that in living as we do, I have failed my daughters by not enabling them to know and experience more. For example, none have experienced (as I didn't) *bat mitzvah*, and perhaps I should have talked that through with them before they go into the world as young Jewish women however secularised they might choose to be. One day one of them might ask me why.'

'But you have always poured love upon them, Elise, and that is the most important *Karuṇā* you can give them.'

'Well, I hope so, and were something to happen to me, I hope I have given them enough to establish their own identity whatever it might be. At least they weren't boys and I might have had to circumcise them!'

'I expect therefore they also are glad not to be boys!'

And by now the girls were no longer children. Already Grace had just left for university to train to be a vet, and Julia and Gale were full of the joys and sometime pains of teenage life. And then came a change that would shake us all to the very depths of our being.

The Return to Silence

I can recall the morning as if it was yesterday, when Elise woke up feeling poorly and being sick. Nothing had suggested this was coming, and at least on that day we just carried on as normal, assuming it was possibly a 24-hour bug but when I looked in to see her, I remember how she looked unwell and an unusual colour, suggestive of jaundice.

On the following day it was clear she was worse, and Pieter took her to see the doctor, Aishe's husband, Tan. He examined her, and immediately asked Pieter to take her to the hospital in Northallerton for tests. On the journey she had been sick in the car three times and when they came home Pieter seemed worried. Elise looked worse and trying to be as composed as she could went straight back to bed.

On the following morning, Pieter called Tan at home, who at once came to the house, from where he called an ambulance to transfer her to hospital as soon as possible. He said he had little idea as yet what the matter was but the way he said it suggested a seriousness which concerned us all.

Elise was subjected to extensive tests and scans and was eventually diagnosed with cancer of the pancreas, and she began to experience back pain and felt constantly sick. She came home after five days, but it was already clear that her treatment was palliative. Tan came in to see her almost every morning. He prescribed medication to help with the sickness and a low dose of diamorphine for the pain, but she said she did not wish to be sleepy, preferring a modicum of pain to endless sleepiness. Unless something wholly unexpected happened we all realised she was going to die, though it was Elise herself who broke the news to Julia and Gale.

Elise insisted that all of us, the children included, should continue to live as normal as possible. Grace came home from university and wanted to remain, but Elise insisted she return, only coming at the weekends.

On a day-to-day basis most of the caring was done by Fiene and myself. Fiene was devastated but ever-present, holding Elise's hands as they chatted about the wonderful years they had all shared together living here in the Dales. Julia and Gale spent as much time as they could with their mum, but most of all Pieter, who had been the gift of grace for her and she for him as she left the five years of silence. This was the second time he was losing a wife to cancer, and he looked absolutely lost. He had wanted to find a locum vet, but Elise maintained farmers only trusted him.

The hospital doctors who had made the diagnosis, and even Tan, who knew her best, would never talk about her dying, but Elise told me she had known she was going to die from the very first day when she felt ill, and told me that for some weeks before she had been having back and tummy pain, together with itchy skin and had noticed she was losing weight but had even welcomed that.

She decided that she wanted neither chemo nor radiotherapy as she knew enough to know that even with those the chances of her long-term survival were small and that the effects of the treatment were likely to be worse than her present symptoms which were under a modicum of control.

'Do you remember,' she said to me, you told me you used to sing the songs of Simon and Garfunkel whilst you were on your long retreat on Holy Isle?'

'Yes, I do,' I replied with a smile.

'I've been remembering the words of their lovely song *The Sound of Silence*. Some of it could have been written for me:

"Hello darkness, my old friend,
I've come to talk with you again
Because a vision softly creeping
Left its seeds while I was sleeping
And the vision that was planted in my brain
Still remains
Within the sound of silence

And in the naked light, I saw
   Ten thousand people, maybe more
   People talking without speaking
   People hearing without listening
   People writing songs that voices never shared
   And no one dared
   Disturb the sound of silence

"Fools" said I, "You do not know
   Silence like a cancer grows
   Hear my words that I might teach you
   Take my arms that I might reach you"
   But my words, like silent raindrops fell
   And echoed in the wells of silence."'

I could not stop myself sobbing as she spoke these words.

'Hey, Lizzie, you of all people, and perhaps you are the only one, who knows that I have no fear entering again into silence. It's a realm I already know well, and I shall be completely safe. And what I wish is that you continue your own practice of silence so that you and I will continue to be together as sisters.'

At that moment she looked towards the candle that she had asked to be brought to her room.

'You know and understand that the darkness and silence are indeed our old friends. I discovered I hadn't been alone when I realised *Shekinah* as I left the five years, and you encountered the same Presence in that dark night of the death of the beautiful baby boy when we had to struggle back through the heavy snow. So why should I fear now? And you must not be afraid either, my beloved sister Soṇā'.

'We both know there is no magic to change what is happening to me and we both know too that *Shekinah* will not deliver me from what is to come and that's why you must continue to be here, for the rest of our family of course, but for those others whom I know can learn so much from you as I have.'

'Oh no,' I said. 'You have ever been *my* teacher and now I must do without you.'

'Jean-Pierre, all those years ago in his hermitage, told me to enter into the silence, and soon after he died, his work done. I want you to go on whether shaven-headed and wearing robes or not, to go on sharing in the silence, and in turn leading others there. We may never know much the world depends on those sharing in the silent song.'

As the days passed, Elise did become more and more drowsy, but asked that I sit in silence with her rather than engaging in speech.

'I shall miss your lovely voice,' I said as we spoke quite near the end.

'It was what began all this, ironically,' she replied quietly. "My voice that so comforted Gail that she could die, and at the end of my five years that made it possible for poor Barbara also to depart this life as she heard me speaking to her. Please take special care of Gale. More than all the others she will need you when the time is right.'

I wanted to ask what she meant, but by now she was asleep once again. Later it would be Gale herself who sought to take care of me.

Elise went from the first day of her illness to death in just seven weeks, and I was glad for her that it was no longer as I could see she was feeling worse day by day though made every effort especially when her daughters were with her.

She died in an afternoon as the sun was going down and its golden rays shining into her bedroom over the Dales she so adored, surrounded by those who loved her. Elise had already asked her oldest friend Leah, who had known her the longest, to recite in Hebrew the Mourner's *Kaddish*, and then in English. All I can remember of it, and which seemed so appropriate for Elise was, "Blessed and praised, glorified and exalted, extolled and honoured, adored and lauded be the name of the Holy One, blessed be He, beyond all the blessings and hymns, praises and consolations that are ever spoken in the world; and say, Amen.'"

This was simply devastating for us all and I think we cried all the tears possible.

Leah asked Fiene and me, as her mother and sister, to help prepare Elise's body for the undertaker to collect. It was both a loving privilege and terrible as all three of us could do it only sobbing as we did so. When the funeral director arrived it was Pieter and Fiene who carried her body to his vehicle.

It is one of the cruellest, though possibly most merciful, aspects of our lives than even after the death of the one we love, life continues relentlessly. Pieter was called out in the night after Elise had died to a cow needing a Caesarean. Fiene too knew that each new day had to be lived and food provided for us all. But that is what life is like. The day after always comes.

On the evening of her death Pieter revealed the wishes that Elise had expressed for what would happen after she died. She wished her body to be cremated early on the following day in Thirsk, without ceremony and no one present. We were all shocked and the children protested. Leah told us that Elise had been clear that she was Jewish and extremely proud to be, and that Jewish tradition said the body should be disposed of at the first opportunity. As a Reform Jew she said she had wished cremation.

'However,' Pieter continued, 'my lovely Elise has asked for a memorial event for us and anyone else who wishes to come to be held in the open air, in the surgery car park. She has asked Lizzie to lead this and to say something direct but simple about Elise, and then lead us all into a ten-minute silence as the best way of honouring her life, but more especially that of the six million of her fellow Jews who had died in the camps of the Holocaust.'

Everyone agreed that although it would be a painful thing to do, we should honour and fulfil Elise's wishes.

It took place on a Sunday, for Jews the first day of week, and I have no idea how many were in church on that morning, but the car park was filled to overflowing.

I had agreed with Pieter what I should say about Elise. People in the town and local community knew that she was Jewish and had been a rabbi, but for almost everyone who came, what they had not known was that Elise had lived as a solitary for five years in complete silence and therefore had no fear of entering into silence now. I could see astonishment written on people's faces, which was further enhanced when I said that Elise had asked that the best memorial possible, both to her and her six million fellow Jews, who were constantly in her remembrance, who had entered into the silence of the death camps of the Holocaust, was that we now spent ten minutes in silence. Of course there was traffic noise, and birds sang and some cows, which for many years she had regularly milked, could be heard, but the quality of the silence over ten minutes was considerable. Pieter ended it by thanking everyone for coming.

Pieter and Fiene had begged me to continue living with them. Early each morning I lit the candle in Elise's room and remained in silence for even up to two hours at a time. I felt so very close to her in that silence, and to *Shekinah*, the Presence.

She had once said to me that almost all religion derived its impetus from the universal longing for survival of death. Jews were an exception in that life after death played little or no part in their living, something she fully accepted for herself.

'Much though I would wish to do so, I shall not be reunited with Jean-Pierre after I die. *Shekinah* does not offer that, but tells me that the Presence that I experience, and which you have known too, Lizzie, is alongside us, not there to reward us, but to show us that our world, even our universe, is not without meaning and purpose, though what that might be no astrophysics will ever be able to tell. The greatest telescopes will reveal more and more but the reality is alongside us, if we can be silent enough, to hear the silent song.'

And then...

Whilst she was ill, I had received an invitation from Bedale High School, which Elise's three daughters attended, to come and speak to the sixth form about being a Buddhist nun. Elise had urged me to accept so I could talk about silence to young people who were increasingly living amidst constant noise. After she died, I decided I would still do it, though Grace was no longer at the school having now gone to university and the others not yet in the sixth form. The school prospectus maintained that their core values are Courage, Commitment and Compassion, and I thought, because of the emphasis upon the last of those values, as a Buddhist committed to *Karuṇā,* I should summon up my own courage and commitment and fulfil the request, even though just a month after Elsie's funeral event and I knew myself still close to tears.

So, I turned up, wearing my robes for once – a usual visual aid or so I thought – and I spoke for a while and then suggested that before questions, we sit in silence for ten minutes. That was when it happened. One of the teachers present, in whom I had already sensed a measure of unease at my presence, stood up and said he objected.

'This is just religious fanaticism trying to manipulate us,' he said,' loudly and aggressively, 'exploiting our emotions by means of the death and bizarre memorial service of that strange Jewish woman who had been locked away for five years, more than likely in a mental institution'

I cannot recall the effect these words had on the young people and other staff members present, because, without giving it a thought I turned to him and, with all the force I could muster, punched him in the face knocking him off his feet and apparently dislocating his jaw! Apparently, and I cannot recall this, I seemed to lose any sense of what was happening and picked up his chair and threw it through a window. Other teachers came to his rescue and tried to restrain me as I hit out at them, allegedly shouting obscenities in what they assumed was a foreign language. I recall only hearing inside myself and shouting out just one word: *Shekinah*. Eventually they overwhelmed me, and the police came and took me to the police station in Northallerton.

From the moment of my arrival, and clearly still in shock, I did not speak to anyone. Even when Pieter came, I could say nothing. This silence was not deliberate – I found myself incapable of speaking! Because of what they assumed to be deliberate failure to co-operate I spent the night in a police cell and was told that I would be up before the magistrates in York once the Crime Prosecution Service had agreed that I could be charged with Actual Bodily Harm. But I never appeared in court as on the following morning a psychiatrist was sent by the CPS to the police station to interview me and to guide them before agreeing to charges. My recollection of what happened is hazy, but I do remember the silly man asking ridiculous questions to which I gave no answers. Apparently, he concluded that I was suffering from Borderline Personality Disorder and recommended I be transferred over to a special Unit in County Durham which dealt with BPD, operated within the confines of the Ministry of Justice, a former country house, but in effect a prison. It took me 24 hours there before I came to and realised something dreadful had happened.

The doctor appointed to meet with me was called Melissa Rivers, a psychiatrist but also a qualified psychotherapist. As soon as we met my seeming inability to speak, technically known as elective mutism, came to an end allowing me to describe over several hour-long sessions, all that my life had contained and how I had managed to find myself in here in this Unit in Upper Teesdale, County Durham. She told me, after I had concluded with the school story that all that happened in the school was the result of a form of post-traumatic stress disorder brought on as the result of the terrible bereavement I had just experienced and extreme provocation by the teacher, but definitely not Borderline Personality Disorder.

'There's definitely nothing wrong with your personality,' she told me.

I enjoyed my sessions with Mel, even when she asked me to consider whether I had fallen in love with Brett and under the influence of that love, become a nun. Perhaps even more daring was her second question.

'Is it possible that what happened is that you later fell in love with Elise, and that was why you wanted to leave Samye Ling and be with her?'

I thought for a while. Did I fall in love with Brett and allowed that love to influence my eventual choice to become a nun?'

'As an 18-year-old I probably did fall for Brett even though I knew he was becoming a monk, and he remained somewhere inside in the following years as I grew into Buddhism, broke up with David and opted for life as a Buddhist nun. That was why, I suppose, I wrote to him to let him know, and was absolutely delighted to receive a reply. It felt like a blessing and that I was drawing near to him. Does than serve as an adequate answer?'

'Our motives for anything are made up of a complex intertwining of influences, most of which are unconscious. Instant conversions of any kind, equally consist of strands of our development to the moment when all appears simple and straightforward but are far from that. Falling in love conversions, no less than religious conversions, are customarily the product of our predisposed conditioning. But what of my second question? Did you fall in love with Elise?'

Again, I thought for a while before answering.

'I came to Elise in the middle of the night. I came to her knowing she was not just Jewish and also a Rabbi but also, as she had told me, that unbeknown to her until much later, she had been baptised as a Catholic at three days old. I urgently need someone to baptise a dying baby and there was chance of getting a minister given the extent of the snow and the distance he would have to come. As someone who had been baptised (however bizarre the circumstances), she could perform the action needed, but why would she? There was not even the slightest moment of hesitation when she said Yes.

'My love for Elise was a response to having witnessed something quite exceptional when she baptised the baby boy and ministered to his parents in their grief so naturally and lovingly. As I drove her back after the ambulance had taken the now dead baby away, I don't think we spoke much, but I knew I had been in the presence of true *Karuṇā*, that which was the end and aim of our Buddhist life.

'How could I not fall in love with her, Mel? And I further believe that if you too had been there, you would have done so too, because what she revealed was what life is all about or meant to be. But she also fell in love with me because we had shared this revelation of *Karuṇā* and *Shekinah*. Only that can explain why it was that without communication she knew I was coming and more or less the day of my arrival. She had even told the others in the house and so when I walked into the kitchen I was greeted by name by Elise's Dutch mother and told that I had been expected.

'Yes, I was in love with Elise but there was never any attempt on my part to make this possessive in any way. It took the form of sharing her life and our common commitment to silence and *Shekinah*, which I have already told you about. But there was more because she shared with me aspects of her experience in her years of silence which she knew from my own experience I would recognise and understand as no one else could. It was truly sisterly love in its affections. I miss her every day, every moment.'

'That's what bereavement is about. How right you were to react as you did in that school. You were in no state to be speaking about Elise and silence publicly so soon after her death, and paradoxically a two-week break up here is exactly what you needed before returning to the normality of your life and practice now without her.'

'But I have to return to court.'

'You can't *return* to court because you didn't go in the first place. The CPS asked for a psychiatric assessment prior to charge. My report will be that there is no charge to answer, that the school failed egregiously in its duty of care towards a visitor, by not preventing a teacher with a clear agenda openly abusing you in front of school children and that you hit out in defence of the reputations of Elise and yourself, and ultimately of two of her children still attending the school, at a time when you were unquestionably suffering from the PTSD caused by the death of someone close whom you loved intensely. Or have I got that wrong?'

'No. It is true.'

'Gosh, I don't often hear that word, either in my work here or in any of my training. Hold on to it. I will speak to them as soon as we finish this morning and add that there is no likelihood you would ever use violence again, and that it should be made clear to the school that they owe you an apology for the distress it has caused you and the family of Elise. Let me do that now and I shall get back to you.'

I had a mug of tea and reflected on my fortnight here. Mel was right. Getting right away had been good but if I was now being set free, I had to face the question of where I would go. I didn't know what sort of stories about me had been doing the rounds locally in the villages of the Dales, and perhaps Pieter would not want me back and maybe I didn't want to go back to community gossip and possible stares. I'm sure mum and dad would welcome me back with open arms. Or should I return to Samye Ling, shave my head and allow my time of freedom to be forgotten?

Mel returned immediately after lunch.

'It took longer than I thought to get through to the CPS in Leeds and they had difficulty locating your case. I told her the full story and made it clear that your mutism was involuntary and that once you were here, there was no difficulty She accepted that there was no case to answer and would inform the police in Northallerton of this decision, meaning you are free. She also indicated that she would write to the school about their failure to exercise proper duty of care to a visitor by allowing the teacher to address you as he did.'

'But what does being free mean?'

'We can order a taxi to take you to Durham and a pass for a train to wherever you wish to go, though probably not Nepal! Or you might possibly consider coming with me to my home this evening and on my day off tomorrow I'll drive you back. It's not that far and I'd be happy to do it. Come to think of it I could you drop you off at my place now and you can phone those you need to and let them know what's happened.'

'Thank you. That is unbelievably generous of you. I didn't bring much so I'm ready as soon as you are.'

'You'll need to sign some papers accepting release from our care and then I'll take you. It's near Barnard Castle so it doesn't take five minutes. I should be back by 6-00 at the latest.'

'I will gladly accept your offer of hospitality, or as I would prefer to call it *Karuṇā*.'

My first call was to Pieter's mobile who was tending to a poorly heifer in Bishopdale.

'I've been completely freed, no charges, and I'll be back tomorrow. One of the doctors will bring me.'

'Where are you? Nobody would tell us where you were.'

'It's a complex story but I'm near Barnard Castle.'

'A complex story involving you? That will make a change, Lizzie,' he replied, laughing.

'I'm freed of all charges, but I wonder whether in the light of everything you would want me back.'

'You're a local hero, Lizzie. The story of what you did has gone round the town and they can't wait to congratulate you. So, there's no question of anything other than coming back to your family. It was bad enough losing Elise without losing you too. Who is there to light the *Shekinah* candle each day if you're not here?'

I put the phone down with tears coursing down my cheeks but got myself together enough to call mum and dad who were hugely relieved to hear from me. Dad said he could come and get me, but I told him that I needed to get back to my work in the surgery and a measure of normality, but that I hoped to get to see them over Christmas before my trip to Nepal.

After work, Mel took me out for a meal in her favourite local restaurant. What did not surprise me, because I recognised the signs, is that she wanted to know more about my experience of silence.

I told her more fully about my own experience of three years, three months and three days, which she said sounded like a prison sentence.

'Oh no, in so many ways it was an experience of liberation from those attachments that hold us back from engaging with the truest and most trustworthy parts of ourselves. Don't forget Elise spent five years in an even greater seclusion and said it took the first three years of that time, in which she would sit in her tiny room without any distraction for four hours a day, to free herself from the ideas, opinions and learning which she felt had clogged up her mind. That was when, as far as I can understand, *Shekinah* was first experienced by her in the silence, even though it took two further years for her to know that retrospectively.'

'I'm full of learning of all sorts, full of opinions and views which are often contradictory and confuse me,' said Mel. 'What can those like myself with busy professional lives do to clear away at least some of the junk I carry about in my head?'

'I have experienced great compassion and understanding from you, Mel, what Buddhists call *Karuṇā*. I think it means that your heart is open even if at times there is so much going on in your head that you feel it is closed. You told me the other day that you spent time working in Ashworth Special Hospital with highly dangerous people. You are a special person, and perhaps serendipitously, through a brief encounter with a wayward Buddhist nun, you are asking yourself important questions about how you live the rest of your life. I imagine that will mean continuing in the job you clearly enjoy but perhaps it might mean something new as well, something that enables you to be fed by beauty and silence and to which you might feel you can give yourself totally when you recognise the time has come to complete your working life. But the death of my beloved Elise is before me now as a reminder that life may be short for any of us, and today is, and I'm sorry to use such a hackneyed platitude, the first day of the rest of our lives, which may always be shorter than we imagine.'

'I met an old priest once who told me that maturity consisted in being able to see the truth in platitudes.'

I could tell throughout the rest of our meal that she was thinking hard somewhere inside herself, and my hope was that it was with the right side of her brain that she was doing it.

Returning

I was awake early as usual and sought to spend time in meditation though with so much having happened any hopes I might have had of stilling my head disappeared from the start, and after half an hour I abandoned my attempt.

On the previous evening Mel had suggested we might go for a walk in Upper Teesdale before setting off back home, and I sensed she needed to talk, so although eager to get back home, I was more than happy to agree.

There was, as Elise had often told me, quoting from Ecclesiastes, "A time for speaking and a time for silence" and we observed these naturally as we experienced the countryside that was wilder than I was used to in Wensleydale. As we began our way back to where Mel had left the car, she said, wholly unexpectedly, 'I'm long overdue a holiday and even a sabbatical. Do you think you could use a doctor travelling with you in Nepal?'

I stopped and turned towards her.

'I won't ask you if you mean that, because it's clear to me you do. As someone already with an understanding of *Karuṇā*, how could I not be thrilled to share that with you? The only thing I've set up is a flight from Heathrow to Kathmandu on January 12th. If you can get a seat on that flight, we could travel together.'

'The thing is,' said Mel, once more walking, 'I spent a great deal of last night thinking about all you said during the evening. What a guide you would be, and I would love to visit the monastery where you knew Jampa, and to visit Hilepani, and possibly also go with you to Kanchenjunga. I need to have my brain shaken and all you have told me about Nepal has moved me greatly.'

'And I think it might be hugely advantageous having you as my companion as I return to the place where my Buddhism was born. I hope you can cope with that.'

'I'm not sure what that would mean, but if you want to get up at 5:00 each morning and sit in the full lotus position for an hour, I promise I will try not to disturb you with my snoring as I sleep on!'

We laughed.

'Mel, nothing would give me greater pleasure to do this with you because I am loving every moment we have been able to spend together. It was after all your presence that opened my mouth again after the trauma of my school visit.'

'And I know, Lizzie, there is so much I can learn from the depths of your wisdom and experience, as well as that of Elise through you. She was obviously something very special and that lives on in you. For me it can only mean gain! And, oh yes, I love being with you too!' she added with a grin.

'You only just got that in on time,' I responded.

As we drove to Wensleydale she told me a little about her own journey to the present.

'After school I read Classics at Cambridge, and then changed to sciences and trained to be a doctor before specialising in psychiatry at the Maudsley Hospital in London. For some reason I chose to specialise in forensic psychiatry, wanting to understand more about people do the things they do, some of them so terrible. Eventually I went to work as a senior psychiatric consultant at the Ashworth Special Hospital on Merseyside working with some of the country's most dangerous offenders, most of whom had life tariffs, meaning they would die in prison. Whilst there I also undertook the six-year part-time training as a psychotherapist and had a small private practice. That was when I first met my colleague Christy, who'd pursued a similar career to my own and worked at Broadmoor and Rampton before becoming Director here.

'I left Ashworth to care for my dying mother, and then my dad, who died less than a year later, which gave me a first opportunity to engage in end-of-life care.

'After mum and dad died, Christy approached me and suggested I join her here within the Department for Justice, specialising in referrals from the justice system where a diagnosis of borderline personality disorder had been given by resident prison psychiatrists. Some of those who came were trying simply to "play the system" and attempt early release, spending time in what was regarded as something of a cushy number compared with prison, though we are both more than accomplished at recognising the signs, and a significant proportion of our patients are back in their referring prisons in less than a week. I have sought to work with my therapeutic rather than my psychiatric skills, making far less use of drugs which have often been given to difficult prisoners to lessen their behavioural difficulties.'

I listened fascinated as she spoke about the privilege of working with some of their patients through the complexities of their lives in the hope that behaviour patterns could be better understood and attended to.

'Do you ever come across people who are genuinely suffering from psychiatric disorders and don't lend themselves to the sort of help you provide.'

'Oh heavens, yes. And once again, Christy and I can usually spot these people almost at once and we must return them back to the prisons from which they came, occasionally recommending a transfer to one of the Special Hospitals. And then, there are the patients who are sent to us for no reason other than that the psychiatrist is wholly at a loss, some of whom are either awaiting pre-sentencing or pre-Parole Board reports, and some who simply have been caught in unfortunate circumstances.'

'Like me?'

'Yes, but more complex than you, the victims of abuse, sexual and non-sexual, coercive behaviour and even in one instance with a patient I knew well, the result of the appalling bullying by the church of one of its own priests that compounded his experience of emotional and physical abuse by his mother.'

'It might be said,' I commented, 'that I am here because my mum and dad were simply wonderful and allowed me always to be myself. Perhaps if they had been more controlling, none of what has happened to me would have come about.'

'But did the circumstances of your life just "come about"? Do you feel the helpless victims of circumstance? I very much doubt it."

'No, you're quite right though I recognise, and how could I not, from our previous conversations the powerful influence that circumstances and people have on us, but I still own to a certain degree of free will.'

Mel laughed.

'I think that anyone who could manage the long retreat you made without going mad must have considerable reserves of mental strength and courage.'

'I so wish you could have known Elise, for she had a super-abundance of both.'

'I hope I can meet her husband, her mother and her children.'

'I'm sure you will. Julia was named by Elise after Pieter's first wife who died of cancer. Apparently when she was younger she looked more like Pieter but to see her now is to see almost exactly how Elise looked, and her younger sister, Gale, is already showing signs of an intensity of relationship with Elise's spiritual endeavours.'

'Once I'm home I will see if I can book a seat on the same flight as yours.'

'Oh Mel, that is so exciting. I'm sure we will both find it a journey of discovery in so many ways, if we survive the bus journeys, and if you think I'm joking, trust me, I'm not!'

A Second Coming

As I walked through the front door I heard a familiar voice from the kitchen.

'It will be Soṇā.'

'It is, it is,' I replied laughing and throwing my arms around Fiene. 'Those were the words you said at my first coming, and I am back.'

'What a good job I've just made a Dutch cake and I expect you will give a warm welcome to a mug of Yorkshire tea.'

I introduced Mel to Fiene and Pieter who had come home early to welcome me back.

'Thank so much for taking good care of Lizzie,' said Fiene.

'I'm just so sorry it added to the existing burden of your loss of Elise. It was so unnecessary, but I've learned a great deal from Lizzie about Elise and it's clear she was one of the most special people in our world, and I cannot imagine what your sense of loss must be.'

'Having to attend to my mama and the children, plus a demanding job on the farms each day,' said Pieter, 'can serve as quite an anaesthetic, but there have been moments when I have stopped the van somewhere we both loved and simply sobbed. I know for certain that if anyone had said to me what the teacher at Bedale School said to you, Lizzie, I would have shattered his jaw, not just dislocated it. That was evil, and we are so indebted to you, Mel, for helping the lawyers see straight. I've already told you, Lizzie, that in the town you are regarded as a hero. Elise was loved and respected across the community and people were outraged when it was learned what he had said, and that it was you and not him who was arrested.'

'But it will be important for us as a family',' added Fiene, 'to have you back. It feels as if on top of losing Elise, we've also lost the other rock on whom we depend.'

'I'm so looking forward to seeing everyone again,' I said. 'I'm no hero, but it's wholly thanks to Mel's wisdom and love that I'm free again.'

'Just doing my job,' she said with a large wink to Pieter.

'I just want to show Mel Elise's room before she has to head back as I have told her so much about it, but I'm sure once we've done that a piece each of one of your cakes and a mug of tea will be just what the doctor ordered, isn't that right, doctor?'

Mel grinned, and I led her into Elise's study.

'It has a lovely atmosphere,' she said, 'and unless I'm mistaken that smell is beeswax. *Shekinah?*'

'The candle has been waiting for my return, but yes, Elise always preferred beeswax candles.'

I took out the matches from a drawer and lit the candle.

'I'm possibly being superstitious,' said Mel, 'but the atmosphere in the room is almost such that I can touch it.'

'It's not contrived; it's real.'

We remained standing in silence for almost five minutes before I gently took Mel's hand and led her to the kitchen and cake and tea.

'Loss can be terrible,' said Mel to Pieter, 'and for you this is a second loss.'

'I was enabled to recover from the death of Julia when I met Elise, but I think less of loss than the gain. I loved Julia but we were together for such a short time. I was granted the joy of Elise for many wonderful years, and have my Grace, Julia and Gale, and my dear mama, together with Lizzie, to continue enjoying what she gave us and upon which we shall continue to feed for the rest of our lives. I cry for my loss of course, and we all do, but far greater would have been our loss had we not had her with us for so long.'

I was suddenly struck by something.

'Who's milking the goats?' I said.

He grinned.

'Yes, Elise would want practical matters to be attended to before too much maudlin conversation. Julia has taken it on and even now has plans to increase the size of the flock. Already she has her sights set on Agricultural College, though who will look after the goats then, I couldn't say.'

'I told Mel that in many ways she's the one of the three most like Elise in looks.'

'Yesterday morning, when I went out, I saw her attaching teats to one of the nannies with her back to me and for a moment I was convinced it was Elise.'

I smiled and nodded.

'I see Elise in all three girls, Pieter,' I said.

'The girls are due back from school at any moment, but earlier Julia telephoned with news. The head had called Gale and her to see him, and told them that Mr Fullwood had been suspended and will not be returning to the school, and that the Chair of the Governors wishes to come and see Lizzie and the whole family to offer apologies for what happened for which the school was taking full responsibility. Julia also added that the head had said Fullwood might be investigated by the police for making an anti-Semitic remark in front of the school.'

'Well, Mel,' I said, 'This is all your doing. I will certainly try never to get on the wrong side of you!'

We all laughed and heard the front door opening with a burst and in came Julia and Gale who threw themselves at me.

'Have you heard the news about the school getting rid of Fullwood and you're not to blame at all?' said Julia.

'Yes, your dad has just told me. Isn't it amazing?'

'Not really,' said Gale. 'Everybody knows you were just defending mum. We think you're wonderful and it's smashing having you back.'

'That's because of this lady, Dr Melissa Rivers. She got me out and brought me home and has been dying to meet you.'

'Lizzie told me all about you and your other sister, but especially about your lovely mum. You have lost a great deal, but she has given so very much in the way of riches you will never forget. But now I must get back to my own home as it is getting dark. What a joy it has been meeting the people I've been hearing so much about!'

I went outside with Mel.

'You said wonderful things in there. Thank you.'

'I am leaving you somewhat reluctantly because I have received so much from you, but when I get home the first thing I will do will be to book that plane!'

'Keep in touch,' I said as we hugged one another.

Once I was back in the kitchen, Julia said, 'We're so pleased to have you back, Lizzie. It means that things are a bit more normal.'

'And I hear you are now the official goatherd.'

'Do you think mum would be pleased?'

'Pleased? She would be over the moon.'

'Raj has begun helping Julia now too,' said Gale, causing Julia to blush just a little.

'That's not exactly a surprise, I said, adding to Julia's blushes, 'but how I have longed to see you all again. It's felt like a lifetime.'

'Lizzie, there is something we all need you to do,' said Fiene. 'Since you left there has been no one to light Elise's candle and keep it burning. She would want you to do that.'

'I have already done so and each morning when I go into her room I shall light it.'

'I think it will help us know mum is still with us,' added Gale.

'Or more likely, that we are with her,' I replied.

After hearing accounts of what had happened to me after the incident in school, the girls' attention inevitably turned towards food. It was Friday evening and they had decided that they must keep the Friday evening ritual, as two of them were Jews. Shortly before we began, presided over by Julia, the telephone rang, and it was Grace calling from her hall of residence to welcome me home and wishing she could be here.

'Actually, Lizzie, I've met with a Jewish family and shall be joining them tonight for their Friday evening meal. They do it differently to us, probably the proper way of doing it, but I shall be there with you all.'

I passed the message on as the five of us sat at the table and the candles lit and the words spoken, and the bread broken and the cup shared. Oh, how I missed Elise!

Gale

It was the weekend and I struggled to leave my comfortable bed to go downstairs on the Saturday morning, light the candle and sit on the floor, but eventually did so. Afterwards, and before I left to have some breakfast, I noticed a piece of paper I hadn't seen before, sticking out of the *Diary of Etty Hillesum* which I knew Elise had been reading before she became unwell. She had copied some words out:

"...Take me by Your hand, I shall follow You dutifully and not resist too much. I shall evade none of the tempests life has in store for me, I shall try to face it as best I can....I shall never again assume in my innocence, that any peace that comes my way will be eternal. I shall accept all the inevitable tumult and struggle. I delight in warmth and security, but I shall not rebel if I have to suffer cold, should You so decree. I shall follow wherever Your hand leads me and shall try not to be afraid. I shall try to spread some of my warmth, of my genuine love for others, wherever I go."

I wept as I read, not least because I knew from where the bookmark was placed that they must have been some of the last words Elise ever read and had clearly taken for her own but also because I knew that for Etty Hillesum, the "wherever I go" was to her murder in Auschwitz with other Jews on 30 November 1943.

I shared these words with Fiene as we ate out porridge together.

'Both Elise and Etty Hillesum, of whom I had heard many years ago back in the Netherlands, followed the hand that led them to death, and both were full of love. Thinking back, Lizzie, I can't get over how much love Elise showed us in the days of her dying, almost as if she were the one caring for us. I miss her so terribly much because she was my daughter and children should never die before their parents.'

'You were her mother, for the woman who gave birth to her and deprived her of the knowledge of her Jewish identity was no mother at all.'

'You are off to Nepal in January, and whilst I am glad for you to have the opportunity to return, I shall miss you here, as I have in the past couple of weeks. You will come back, won't you?'

'Oh yes. Just being back here feels perfect. It is my true home, even though I love my mum and dad. I've said I shall try to get there for Christmas.'

'Why don't you invite them to come and spend Christmas with us. Your mum and I get on so well and it would enable them to spend time with you without the rest of the family. You deserve others caring for you, Lizzie, after all you've been through.'

'Perhaps you should ask Pieter if he agrees.'

'He will do what his mama tells him,' she said, with a smirk.

The man himself entered the kitchen.

'What will he do, mama?' he asked with an impish grin.

'Have Lizzie's mum and dad here for Christmas.'

'Oh yes, please,' said Pieter

'Poor Grace,' I said. 'It will mean having to share her room with me.'

'Don't worry about that. Now she's at vet school I'll ensure she works so hard over the holiday, she'll sleep so well she won't notice you in the other bed. Besides she's longing to see you. She says she wants to thank you personally for hitting Mr Fullwood.'

'Oh dear, what a reputation as a peace-loving and non-violent

Buddhist I am acquiring.'

'Aishe is coming to see you this morning and will be bringing Raj with her. Ever since they were at school together, he and Julia have been close friends and still are.'

'And tomorrow,' added Fiene, 'Leah and Ursula are coming for a non-kosher Sunday lunch. You are much in demand, but you mustn't allow people to overwhelm you. You will perhaps need your time in Nepal as a kind of solitary retreat.'

'I'm looking forward to it, but it won't be solitary. I'm not travelling alone. Dr Rivers is hoping to accompany me.'

'She sounds exactly the right sort of company for you. A psychiatrist, I mean!' said Peter.

'Thank you, Pieter, for that profound insight!'

We laughed.

I called mum and dad immediately after breakfast and they leapt at the chance to come for Christmas. Mum said helping Fiene would be a real treat.

Aishe and Raj arrived shortly before 10:00 and she just about knocked me down with her hug.

'Oh Lizzie, I'm so overjoyed to have you back. We are all so proud of your newly acquired pugilistic skills. Raj says Fullwood was useless as a teacher, so you did a great service to the children of the school. And I must tell you how much Tan was affected by his times with Elise, even to the extent of wondering if he has too scientific a mind all these years and has now begun to take my meditation seriously.'

'Oh Aishe, how Elise would laugh to know that, but has her death affected you, other than the grief we all feel?'

'In terms of meditation, do you mean?'

'Yes, but not just that.'

'How could any contact with Elise, including our loss of her, not affect all of us. I've sometimes gone up the hill where the horses train, a place I know she loved. Being there has made me cry but I've had a sense of what she was about in some mysterious way I don't understand, and telling me not to look at her but at the hills up the dale and allow myself to be moved more by them.'

'I hope I shall have the courage to go up there too. I recall picnics and walks up there, talking about nothing as we loved to do, and then listening as words of wisdom flowed out of her.'

'Yeah, but you're not short of courage, so don't imagine we're not looking to you to continue her work, because we are, and a couple of those who come to your meditation group are desperate to get going again.'

We were sitting in Elise's room and Aishe pointed to the candle.

'*Shekinah*, the Presence, was with her throughout, not working magic but there alongside her. I wish some of those clergy we met at Butlin's could have been here because Elise showed us how to die as well as how to live, not just rescue a crippled religion in its death throes.'

'Blimey,' I said, 'Elise's death has certainly energised you.'

'Yes, it's odd but I think it has. And are you still going to Nepal after Christmas? They've really missed you here, you know.'

'Yes, I realise that, but I think it will be a source of strengthening and renewal. It's not a long trip. They'll manage without me here, but please say nothing about what I'm going to tell you. I intend asking Gale if she will take responsibility for the candle each day. Grace is going to be a vet; Julia wants to do farming and looks like Elise the most; but in Gale I have perceived something special, nearer to the heart of the Elise we knew. They won't be alone here.'

Leah and Ursula came on the Sunday for lunch (definitely their primary reason for coming, though they would have denied it!) to see how I was after my imprisonment. Ursula was interested to know whether I thought the interruption of Fullwood had contained an element of anti-semitism.

'Yes, it did.'

'It's not an important point, though,' added Pieter, 'after all we've had Grace through the school whom he would have taught and now Julia and Gale are there, so it's quite likely he would have known they are Jewish. When the Chair of Governors comes to see us, I will raise it with her.'

'Dad, I don't want you to,' said Julia. 'Me and Gale are proud to be Jewish and nobody has ever given the slightest sign that it's a problem, and Grace never mentioned anything. To bring it up isn't what I would want.'

'Nor me, dad,' added Gale. 'Like Julia I'm right proud to be Jewish and maybe one day like Grace is doing, I will want to take it further, as mum did only when she found out when she was 19. I don't want to stand out when at school though I like the way mum has brought us up to love what we do on Fridays and at Hannukah.'

'Well,' said Leah, 'anyone who's "right proud" is also well and truly Yorkshire as well.'

Gale did not blush but laughed with the rest of us. I was sure I was right about her being closest to Elise.

By Monday I was back in my practice routine after lighting the candle and engaging in some Tibetan singing before meditation. I was due to return to work following lunch, but after breakfast I went back to my own room looking out of the window over the valley and began to ask myself just what I thought *Shekinah* meant to me as a Buddhist.

Buddhism had been and I presumed still was for me the guiding light, as it had been for me over the previous years of total involvement, until I met Elise. The encounter in the night, as I increasingly thought of it, had turned my ideological commitments somewhat upside down, not least because encountering Elise also meant encountering *Shekinah*, and it didn't fit.

Elise had never asked me to make it fit and indeed had asked nothing of me other than continue my practice but that was easier said than done when there was evidence staring me in the face that to this woman *Shekinah* was real. To dismiss that, as my Buddhism would demand, as it posits belief in no divinity or god (this side of death, anyway, and thereafter only in speculation drawn from native Tibetan religions), would be to question the integrity of Elise herself.

On the previous evening, I had been reading more of the *Diary of Etty Hillesum* whose own encounter with God (and she uses that word over and over), convinced me that she had what is called mystical union.

I had sat back and began to consider whether this described Elise, that she was, as such, a mystic, one who knew the almost corporeal reality of the divine within. But I knew she had neither said nor even suggested it, and her Jewish self would have found it hard even to accept the possibility.

Elise rejected all talk of and refused to use the G word and all talk of beliefs about such a possibility but from her five year sojourn in silence, she emerged not alone but with *Shekinah*.

It was obvious to anyone that Elise was one of the sanest people ever, never wanting to speak or show off this central reality of her life. Fiene and Peter had long since accepted the little she had said, because she said so little and was wholly matter of fact about it, at once distinguishing her from the mass of religious people in history who obsessively need to tell others about their faith, needing to justify it to themselves, which is why they seek converts. It was not so with Elise.

Etty Hillesum took her intense awareness of God's presence with her into Auschwitz to be with others as she too awaited murder in the gas chambers at the age of just 29. Elise was in her 50s when she died of cancer. Clearly *Shekinah* was no protection against the vicissitudes of existence, which many religious people hope their faiths provide. I knew very little about mystics in the various religious traditions but enough to know that very often they experienced suffering and difficulties. And yet, Etty Hillesum and Elise, both members of the most despised race in history, could not, nor wished to, deny what they knew.

I was facing a challenge.

In the following week I asked 14-year-old Gale to join me for a chat in her mum's room. I had seen her entering several times.

'Do you like your mum's room?' I asked.

'Yes. I feel so very close to her in here and now you're back her candle is lit and I'm so pleased about that.'

'You know that I'm going to be in Nepal and India for three weeks in January?'

'You don't have to; and we don't want you to. You've been away already, and we missed you so much.'

'Well, I probably do have to, not least because when I talked it over with your mum, she encouraged me to set it up. But I've been giving thought to the days when I'm away. Perhaps you might come in each morning and light mum's candle.'

'I would like to do that, but what about the others, would they want me to?'

'Provided you blow it out before you go to bed and the house doesn't burn down, I think they would like you to do that.'

'What about Julia? Shouldn't she do it too?'

'Julia has inherited your mum's goats and love of farming. I think you may have inherited something else.'

Gale has beautiful large eyes, and they widened now.

'Yes. I know, even though I don't know what I know.'

'That's the most important thing – not claiming to know what you don't and perhaps can't ever know but knowing that you do know something important.'

'Mum called it *Shekinah* and explained something of what it means: Presence, being here.'

'Did she ever tell you why you are called Gale?'

'Wasn't there a gale blowing when I was born, though there was something else she said she would tell me about one day but wasn't able to?'

'There *was* a gale blowing as you entered the world, but your name had a far deeper meaning for her. It was just after she had realised she was a Jew, and she worked as a volunteer at the Samaritans.'

'I've heard of them. They're a sort of Childline for grown-ups.'

'Yes. Well one night a young woman called in. The woman's name was Gail, spelt with an I, and she had already deliberately taken an overdose of drugs with which to kill herself and she wanted your mum, as you and I both know her to have had so lovely a voice, to continue talking to her as she died. Your mum asked if she wanted help, but Gail wanted to die and the Samaritans have always said that if this is their choice, they must be allowed to do so.'

'Did she die?'

'Well, two days later your mum heard a report on the news that a young woman called Gail and been found dead in a flat, together with her baby.'

'A baby? Did mum not know about that?'

'No. Gail had said nothing about a baby. Had she even hinted that she had a baby your mum would have sent out help at once. But Gail's death and that of her baby remained with her throughout the five years she spent alone, and other deaths too, and so when you were born, it was almost as if something special had happened and that something in the world had been put right even, for Gail and her baby.'

Gale had tears running down her cheeks.

'Mum never said anything about these things.'

I then told her the story of how the baby had died but not before Elise had baptised him.

'She baptised a baby! But she was Jewish.'

'Yes, but when she was just three days old, she had been baptised by a Catholic priest called Fr Jean-Pierre, and only someone who has been baptised can do the same for another. I asked her if she would and she said yes, without a thought. It was infinite love in action, what Buddhists call *Karuṇā*, Great Compassion.

'I am certain that she knew that on that terrible night in which Gail and her baby died, *Shekinah* was there too, and perhaps always is for all of us. It's just that most of us seem completely unable or unwilling to grasp the reality.'

'Is that the same for you, Lizzie? Do you experience the Presence?'

'You know that I'm a Buddhist nun, and Buddhist theory does not accept that *Shekinah* can be possible. Your mum did not want to stop me continuing as a Buddhist because I suspect she knew that any huge change is best done bit by bit, and since coming to live with you that's what I've been doing.'

'I remember coming into the kitchen when you first got here to see your bald head.'

I laughed.

'Yes, hair is definitely useful in Wensleydale in winter.'

'So, are you not a Buddhist now?'

'To answer that question is the most important reason why I need to go back to Nepal where it all began.'

'You'll have your doctor friend with you, so I hope she won't let you shave your head!' said Gale giggling.

'I think she's also on a journey of exploration, but even without her I shan't be alone, will I?'

Gale looked at the candle.

'No, you won't. But what I don't understand is why my awareness of *Shekinah* doesn't seem to make me better as a person. I still think horrible things about people, and I deliberately tripped up one of the players in hockey the other afternoon.'

I smiled.

'It took your mum five years of solitude and silence to grasp it, but *Shekinah*'s not like the way most people think of a god, which is why it's almost impossible to speak of it to anyone as they would confuse it with all they think belief in god consists of, always looking down to find out if we're naughty or nice, like Santa Claus all the year round. It's completely different. And whether we're lucky enough to have this awareness is neither here nor there. You mum always said it's like being Jewish or having that beautiful brown skin of Raj and his mum – it's just there. I think the next time she comes you should talk about this with Leah. She's known of this since she was your age too and you can trust her.'

'I trust you, Lizzie.'

'And I've learned a great deal from you in our conversation in this past hour, just as every moment in your mum's presence was a gift to me.'

'Yes, and now we have to live without her.'

There were tears again.

'Like you I cry a great deal because of my loss, but I console myself knowing she was not even slightly afraid of entering the silence again.'

'Because of *Skekinah*, you mean?'

I smiled and touched her hand.

'Who knows?'

She smiled back.

Hannukah and Christmas

As Hannukah and Christmas approached I casually mentioned to Fiene and Pieter that I had suggested Gale might like to light the candle in Elise's room in my absence. If I had anticipated objections on the grounds of safety there were none, almost as if they too realised a bond between Gale and Elise.

'It will be less smelly than Julia and the goats,' said Pieter.

'Huh,' replied his mum, 'Pot verwijt de ketel dat hij zwart ziet.'

I looked bemused at this rare lapse into Dutch in my presence.

'Mama has just told me it is a case of the pot calling the kettle black! Ok, so I sometimes bring in the odours with which I work all the time.'

'Somtijds?' replied Fiene.

Pieter laughed and I needed no translation.

'Grace will be home next week and she'll be out with me most days. You won't complain about her.'

'Of course I won't, because my first-born grandchild bears a wonderful name to which she is ever true!'

'I'll go and have a shower,' said Pieter, once again defeated by his mama.

Mel called me to say she was due to go to Newcastle for a meeting and had asked what clothing she should shop for there.

'January can be cold at nights, but during the day it will be ok. You'll need wool and thick cotton, though as we're having it easy staying in hostels and hotels you probably won't freeze. And we shall be there for *Maghe Sankrati*, the harvest festival in which people take a dip in the freezing river to prepare for the auspicious month of Magh.'

'Is it compulsory?'

I could almost hear her teeth chattering in dread and I laughed.

'It's alright, they don't insist on wimps taking part.'

'Will you?'

'You once said you thought I had courage, but trust me, Mel, I'm not crazy. I'll happily join you and other wimps watching the others in the waters that have come down from the Himalayas so cold they can hardly breathe. But of course, I won't stop you if you insist.'

'Naturally I would, but it wouldn't be fair showing you up.'

'Oh, I understand, thank you so much for the sacrifice!'

It was good to have Grace back from university and true to his word, Pieter insisted she join him on the farms, but she said she also wanted to work with Heidi, Fran and myself. As I was taking three weeks away in January, I was working full-time to allow Meredith a break before she had to do the same for me. A veterinary practice like ours covered a huge area. The paying part of the work was the small animal practice run by Heidi and Fran, whereas as in the books by James Heriot, getting money out of farmers was never easy. Quite often I was sent by Pieter to charm it out of them as once he had sent Elise.

Increasingly, veterinary practices now were being taken over by large companies and grouped together. Pieter felt that he was sufficiently nearing retirement to want his to continue as an independent practice, and when fees began to increase steeply in other practices, our lower fees brought us in more work. Heidi and

Fran worked hard, and Pieter often joined them for certain operations. They looked up to him and Fran told me that Pieter was an outstanding vet, and I knew they were glad he had plenty of work, so he didn't have a lot of time to think about his loss of Elise. But, inevitably, he did struggle and often suggested I go out with him on a farm visit just to enable him to talk about Elise and weep as he needed to do.

Grace had undergone some sort of change in her first term, though perhaps it was her mum's death midway that precipitated it. She had become good friends with a Jewish family in Liverpool and was now attending synagogue with them. She hadn't returned home fanatical about it, but we all noticed that she was stricter than the rest of us about food and the way she kept shabbat.

'I think it's wonderful,' said Fiene. 'This was the age when Elise discovered that she was Jewish. Perhaps Grace will understand why Elise did not inflict it upon her dad or me and allow her two sisters to remain as they were. Some people of her age when they get something new can be a real pain, but true to her name that is not how it is for Grace.'

'She told me,' I said, 'the family she now visits call her by the Hebrew name of "*Khen*", but when pronounced sounds mostly like "hen" which as a trainee vet she thinks quite hilarious, but that it derives from a Hebrew root for beauty and compassion. I never heard Elise mention that.'

'She did when Grace was born and to be honest, I had forgotten, but how appropriate. When she came after Elise's death, she was still a girl, but it seems to me she has returned a woman. That was Elise's pattern too if I remember aright. I'm looking forward to hearing what Leah will make of her when she comes next week.'

Leah was delighted that Grace had made contact with a Jewish family and was even considering moving in with them for the following term, just as long-ago Elise had moved in with Leah and her family and discovered something of the reality of Jewish life as lived by a family. She was greatly relieved, however, when Grace told her that they were Reform Jews!

Hannukah led up to Christmas this year and mum and dad came south to join us, and dad especially was moved by the lighting of the lights each day. It was almost enough, he told me, to consider becoming Jewish. When I mentioned circumcision, he told me what daughters didn't need to know, that conveniently it had already been done at birth!

Mum and dad took me out for lunch one day and told me that despite having had a daughter who was a Buddhist nun, the greatest impact in terms of understanding the world and their place in it had come from the time they had spent with Elise on their visits. They had been devastated by her death, but I wanted to reassure them that she hadn't been, that she was sad to be leaving those she loved and hoped that she had done enough to let them know how loved they were, but that she had no fear of re-entering silence. It was her constant companion and friend. She had showed us how to die.

Both mum and dad were crying as I told them this, so much so that the head waiter came over to ask if everything was alright, and through his tears dad somehow managed to blurt out that everything was even better than alright. The head waiter had looked to me, as we knew each other slightly, and I had nodded and smiled at him.

Mum and dad stayed through Christmas Day and Boxing Day, before returning north of the Borders to join the rest of the family to whom I sent my greetings. Having them there was probably a good thing because with it being the first Hannukah without Elise it could have been so desperately sad and wasn't.

It was on New Years Eve that I was most taken by surprise. All three girls were intending to stay up to see the New Year in, though I insisted to their amusement that we call it Hogmanay. After our evening meal, Gale came to my room, and I could see she wanted or needed to say something important.

'Lizzie,' she said hesitantly, 'do you think me and you could be together in mum's room when midnight comes?'

'I think that's a wonderful idea, Gale, and I would like nothing more for us to end this tragic year and begin a new year with all sorts of possibilities before us, being together in silence with *Shekinah*. I don't think you need to say anything to your dad or your sisters about it as I think they will understand that you are very close to your mum in this way. But I think it's quite wonderful that you have come and asked me.'

In Yorkshire there was no longer a special Hogmanay programme on tv, though I wouldn't have wanted to watch it, but at about 11:45 I went to Elise's room where I found Gale already sitting, in silence. I said nothing but sat on the floor in my normal meditation position and together we waited for midnight to come and the New Year begin. We heard the cheer from the others watching television and assumed that we could now complete our vigil. We stood and wept and hugged each other, and I found myself wondering just what would lie before this 14-year-old girl who already was showing all the signs of her mother's spiritual perspicacity. It was quite a thought to take with me to my New Year bed.

Most of the following days were taken up with preparation for my trip to Nepal. I needed winter clothes but before I set out to buy new ones, Pieter asked if I would like to take with me some of the clothes that Elise wore when it was cold. There was no hesitation on my part because I knew Elise had good taste in clothes and as a Canadian knew how best to dress in winter.

I also had frequent contact with Mel. She told me she had been abroad a couple of times to Italy and France, where she felt at ease in European terms, and also to Greece as an undergraduate to further her classical studies. Nepal was a different matter altogether for her and she had tried to do some initial reading, but as I told her, nothing really could prepare her for the cultural transition she would need to make inside herself once we were there. As during my time in her unit, I enjoyed our conversations and was looking forward to the three weeks we would spend together.

On January 11 Mel arrived, leaving her car at the surgery, and with great sadness and many tears, Pieter and Fiene drove us to the railway station in Northallerton as we made our way to London and the hotel I had booked for us at Heathrow.

Just before departing I had sat in Elise's room with the candle which Gale had already lit that morning. She had sat with me for a little while before she left for school. I hoped *Shekinah* would remain here and also be with me.

Kathmandu and Beyond

Our flight was early on the 12th and took us via Abu Dhabi and with Kathmandu 4¼ hours ahead of us, it was already late afternoon when we arrived. Heathrow had been relatively warm so once we left the terminal building in Kathmandu, we at once felt the cold. I had recalled that mum and dad had stayed at the Hotel Barahi and we travelled into the city by taxi, Mel constantly amazed by all she saw, pointing first at this and then at something else. I was enjoying seeing her excitement.

The city is westernised in many ways, catering for the hordes of visitors who wanted their home comforts, especially in the way of food. Despite it being winter still, there were many tourists, but I thought two nights of orientation and seeing the sights here would enable to us to adapt.

Our room was comfortable, and the food mostly Nepalese which meant dhal in its various incarnations, though it's possible to discover burger bars scattered about the place for the visitors. By the next morning, after just one meal, both of us were in need of Imodium, of which Dr Rivers had made sure she had brought a store!

By the end of the next afternoon as tourists, we were already exhausted. We had been to a number of temples, but they had done little to enrich me and as we were drinking tea back in the hotel,

Mel asked my feelings about it all.

'When I was here aged 17, I spent very little time in the city, and I shall be glad tomorrow when we get on the bus and head into the rest of the country. This place is like any tourist paradise. It offers what only appears real, but I think it has at least enabled us to get our bearings, to recognise that we are in a different culture because I think what lies before us will be more demanding of our inner selves than we have experienced here.'

'I'm sure you're right, but don't forget I've never been here before and it's new and enticing rather than simply exciting. I guess that's why I wanted to come with you, because I recognise in you something different that moves me, and I want to learn more.'

'Then you must excuse my negativity. Neither of us would have come here just to stay the same, and that's why it won't just be the bus journey tomorrow that's a challenge, and trust me it will be, but we face encountering mountains of many kinds, inner as well as outer, and they will have their effect upon us.'

In the light of events that ensued, perhaps I should have kept my mouth firmly closed.

On the following morning, we headed east on the bus, and it didn't take Mel long to realise that I had spoken truly about the gorges at the side of the road as we snaked along the valley, though most of the time she couldn't take her eyes of the sights of the Himalayan peaks to the north. I had arranged for us to break the journey with an overnight stay at Hotel Peace Haven which brought us much closer to the ordinary Nepalese life I had known in my earlier visit.

'One of the things I noticed in the city was the presence of Hindu temples,' said Mel. 'I wasn't expecting that.'

'There are many Hindus in Nepal and inevitably some syncretism in the ways communities celebrate feast days. No Buddhist in a village wants to miss out on Diwali, and Hindus love to celebrate the Buddha's birthday.'

'Does that not trouble you?'

'When I was here before, I wasn't yet a Buddhist and enjoyed everything on offer. And now, well look at me. Do I look like a rigorous Buddhist nun?'

On the following day, Mel came to see that this part of the journey seemed even more scary than the day before as we twisted and turned on our route into Hilepani, where a wonderful welcome awaited me. I recognised Hanka at once and she had brought with her some of those I had taught and who now came to see me with their own children in the school. It was good also to meet her husband who having retired from the Gurkhas had decided to return to Nepal rather than striving to live and find work in Aldershot, where many former Gurkhas settled. His English was very good.

I introduced Mel to them and avoided mentioning that she was a doctor as had I done so, I could guarantee on the following morning there would be a queue outside her door. Medical facilities in the town had little improved since my earlier visit and she was here for quite different reasons than the practice of medicine.

We intended making Hilepani our base camp, travelling a long way north into the Himalayan foothills, having one brief vision of Everest as the clouds generously parted for a short while. Mel must have taken hundreds of photos and videos and found the sight awesome.

That evening as we sat together in our room (built since Naomi and I had been there) by the fire, she spoke of the sense within in her of feeling being opened up, and the realisation that her head was so full of information and knowledge that the sight of snow-covered peaks towering above us threatened to call into question all human endeavours, however clever they had become, ironically so clever that they almost gave the impression she felt overtaken by them, that she was no longer in charge.

'But in your work,' I countered, 'you're not reliant on technology. You listen, evaluate and often, or so it seems to me, rely on intuition and the non-verbal.'

'That's on a good day. So very often I'm ticking things off a mental chart because I know that after each session, I have to make notes and regularly speak with a supervisor.'

'I've mentioned Iain McGilchrist to you before. He's a psychiatrist and he would say to you that you need to become much more dependent on the use of the right hemisphere, and surely that's what you were doing when you felt awe in the face of the mountains. For me, it's Kanchenjunga that had the effect upon me last time I was here.'

'That surely is what I've been reflecting on, even pursuing, ever since I met a new patient who turned out to be a Buddhist nun in sweatshirt and jeans.'

'Just as once I met a man called Brett, the son of an Australian father and a Nepalese mother, who became a monk, who had much the same effect on me.'

'You must be looking forward to going to whatever the monastery is called.'

'Namobuddha Monastery. Yes, I am, though with trepidation. What shall I find? Perhaps Jampa has returned to Australia or perhaps knowing I have taken vows as a nun might now disapprove of me and send me packing. I just have to wait until the day after tomorrow when I shall find out.

As we clambered down from the bus at Namobuddha Monastery, I could see major changes had taken place and there were signs that more was happening – lots of green bamboo scaffolding. We made our way into the guest area and placed our kit in the room allocated to us, before heading outside to see the place. Unlike visits to temples in Kathmandu, at this time of the year, it was quiet and largely tourist-free. For our first night we were the only resident guests. The food, we were told would be scraps that had fallen off the tables of the monks – I was used to this, but Mel worried about hygiene until I told her it was a euphemism and meant that we eating as they were. It was, it almost goes without saying, variations on a theme of curry, dhal and rice with some tasty Turung bread.

That evening we attended what are called first Amitabha Prayers which was in effect an hour of Buddhist chanting followed by Chenrezik Prayers, which took a further hour and a half, and during which I could sense that Mel was drifting off to sleep. I too was very tired and so took the opportunity to be in bed and asleep by 9:00, and my alarm set to wake me at 4-30 for early morning prayers half an hour later. Meditation was not until 6:30am and would be followed an hour later by breakfast of Tampa Porridge and Turung Bread, which reminded me so much of Fiene's baking.

During prayers began I could not pick Jampa out of the monks and I wondered if my worst fears had been realised and that he had abandoned his monastery. It was only as meditation began and the Sangha began to sing in Tibetan, that I recognised him, and my heart skipped a beat in relief. After that it was hard to meditate as I kept focussing my eyes on him. He looked older of course, as I imagine I would do to him, and from the place where he was seated, I could see he had achieved a certain seniority within the Sangha.

Once meditation had ended, I was determined to try and speak with him as we all left the temple. I waited until he was approaching the door.

'Jampa,' I said.

He turned and looked at me somewhat quizzically.

He replied in Nepalese gently and at once I recalled the gentleness of his voice.

'I imagine you cannot possibly remember me, but I came to stay here many years ago when you were just Brett and I was...'

'...Lizzie,' he interrupted with a gentle smile, 'but then became

Bahuputtika Soṇā of Kagyu Samye Ling. I have been expecting you.'

I was startled and did not know how to reply. Mel waited for me outside the Temple door, and I wish she had remained with me.

'Might it be possible to speak with you about this?'

'We have strict rules about members of the Sangha meeting with visitors, especially female visitors, but I'm sure the abbot will understand why we should speak. I will send a message to you about when and where but please bring your travelling companion with you.'

'I understand,' I said, as we both collected and put back on our footwear. He then walked in the same direction as the other monks and I turned to Mel but said nothing, though later she could see from my face that something significant has just taken place. I remained rooted to the spot, wondering if what he had just said was true. How could he have been expecting me? Why was I here?

Eventually Mel persuaded me to accompany her down to the dining hall where already we were being joined by some day visitors. We filled our bowls, collected a spoon each and sat at a table. She gave me an enquiring look but said nothing.

'That was Jampa,' I said eventually.

'Something happened; I can tell from your face.'

I told Mel what he had said to me.

'I've ceased to be surprised by anything you tell me, and I'm learning to expect the unexpected.'

He said that when we meet, he wishes you to be there too.'

'Me? Why on earth does he want me there. It's you he says he's being expecting.'

'I have no idea, except perhaps possibly as a chaperone. At Samye Ling we had strict rules about any private meeting with a member of the opposite sex.'

'Something happened to me whilst I was alongside you in the Temple, something fundamental that I could not have possibly known before. I mean the depth and height and breadth of Buddhism as it is lived here in its native lands. I suddenly realised the enormity of what you had done in your retreat of three years and three months and three days and the nature and extent of what you left behind to go to live with Elise. I've often enough come across western young people claiming to be Buddhists, but they don't know the half, and I realised that I don't know the half about you. And then I realised I don't know the half about me.'

I looked up at her.

'Good stuff this porridge,' I said.

She nodded and gave me a broad smile.

'You did say it was a journey of exploration,' she said.

Künshi

The great advantage of being the only two visitors was that in the dormitory we could talk without anyone else hearing.

'I was deeply moved by the chanting before meditation,' said Mel, 'even though I have no idea of what they were chanting.'

'It was in Tibetan and one or two of the older members of the Sangha at Samye Ling had originally come over the mountains to escape from the communists, through whom we all learned enough Tibetan to chant. They are what I would call "settling prayers".'

'But prayers to whom? I thought there are no gods.'

'You're right but these prayers nevertheless invoke blessings from wherever there might be forces or energies for good in the world, just as Buddhists believe that prayers written on the prayer wheels and flags send out blessings across the earth. I continue the practice at home and Elise loved to hear them before we sat in silence together afterwards. She once compared prayers to our need to shout at our tv screens when watching sport. They actually achieve nothing at the match but make us feel better. Perhaps that's what those prayers are about. They work, if that is the right word, on us.'

'That's a great way of thinking about it.'

'And how did you find an hour of silence?"

She made a noise between a grunt and a laugh.

'I heard no silence, just a million voices in my head and I acquired a painful bottom, but if I had been cross-legged as you were, I would have cried out in pain.'

'I have been doing it for a long time. And a sore bottom and a million voices is exactly what I might have imagined you would be experiencing. Stilling those voices took Elise the first three years of her five in total silence. For the other two she had accomplished something extremely rare in Buddhist philosophy.'

'What about you?'

'I remain a striver.'

'Even after your own long silent retreat?'

'Well, let's just agree that on one snowy night with Elise, I witnessed *Karuṇā,* and things changed for me, in the sense that I heard new elements in the silent song and I'm still trying to catch its harmonies.'

'What an amazing thing for me to hear.'

'Why?'

'Because the aspect of your being that makes the greatest impression on me is your stability, your capacity to hold to what you know. And the more you have told me about Elise, the more I recognise you in your descriptions of her. It's because you say so little about so much, and as Fiene and Pieter with Elise, the more I'm inclined to accept all you say.'

'I should never be confused with Elise.'

'I disagree, Lizzie. Might it just be that as Elise was handed the torch by her Canadian priest, so you were drawn to be with her to receive it as she died?'

'So what am I doing here?'

'I know you are not here to gain permission or even approval. I'm seriously impressed by what is here, but I think you've moved on in ways that are no less a total commitment than those of your monastic vows. My knowledge of the Old Testament is limited but what I do remember from the 40 years of the Hebrews in the wilderness is that they were not static. Wasn't it a cloud by day and a pillar of fire by night that led them, however slowly? *Shekinah* may be constant but not static.'

I was stunned by these words from Mel, and I suddenly burst into tears and reached out for her hand, but she came and put her arm around me.

'Perhaps we've come all this not for you to see Jampa, but for. me,' she said. That would soon prove prophetic.

I heard nothing all morning and we wandered about the grounds of the monastery until lunch was served in the dining hall. That was when a young monk came and passed me a note: "The abbot says we can meet in the teaching hall for a short time at 3:00". I showed it to Mel.

'Good, or do I mean something quite other?' she said, mysteriously, though I chose not to pursue it. We both needed a sleep before we met Jampa.

The hall was small enough for an intimate conversation and on arrival we found Jampa already there with two chairs set out for us.

'You said you were expecting me. How could that possibly be?'

'Your abbot at Kagyu Samye Ling wrote to our abbot asking whether it was possible that you might be here. He recalled the message that I had sent at the time of your ordination and said that you had left the monastery still claiming to be a nun. He had decided not to cast you out of the Sangha but to allow you mendicant status until such time as you renounced your vows. He clearly continues to think highly of you and told us that you had recently completed the long retreat but had come under the influence of a guest with whom you had shared a moment of immense significance.

'As for expecting you, I cannot say much because I don't know how, but I had the realisation towards the end of last year, so I have been looking out for you.'

'I'm astonished that my abbot at Samye Ling has not banished me but I remain committed to my vows of Refuge as much now as when I became Bahuputtika Soṇā, even if I have shed what I think of as incidentals which may get in the way of others perceiving what it means for me to be a consecrated nun.'

'There are many Tibetans, don't forget, who still think women cannot be part of the Sangha, but I am not one, though I would ask whether shedding what you call incidentals is not also cutting yourself off from the traditions which have fed us for 2,500 years? There is something in the west now apparently called religionless Buddhism or some such title. Is this something to which you now subscribe?'

'No. That is something alien to me and my practice but is typical of the western frame of mind that seeks to say that everything must be up-to-date, modernised to fit the way the so-called influencers seek to determine how we think. They cannot see that there will be days to come when we shall need to call upon our resources from the past to enable us to survive. It's called reductionism but really it's the destruction of our treasures upon which we still depend. I face an uncertain personal future. The guest the abbot spoke of has died and I'm far from certain what to do now.'

He smiled.

'Then you should be glad,' he said. 'Am I not correct in thinking that our brief, and they were very brief encounters, led you to Samye Ling?'

I looked at Mel.

'Yes,' I replied.

'Then you have come back just in time.'

Jampa turned to Mel.

'And why are you here? I don't just mean in this hall here and now. If you know Soṇā as she is, and I have just heard how she is, your presence is not merely a coincidence.'

'I have achieved a great deal,' she said. 'I had an outstanding academic career, became a doctor, a psychiatrist and trained as a therapist. I hold a senior position in a government hospital working with troubled men and women. Since meeting with Lizzie, I began to realise that I was like a posh motor vehicle, shiny and admired by all, but running on empty. This morning during meditation, I realised that all these things were serving not to enhance me but preventing me, though I'm still far from sure I know what it is preventing me from.'

Jampa smiled at her, and then looked away from us both and paused before speaking again.

'Our friends the Hindus speak most about karma. When I was young and growing up in Australia, I shared the culture of drinking and smoking. At college I smoked heavily and did so until I came to live here. My chest was not good, but I felt the clear air here would cleanse my lungs. But the damage it would appear has been done, and I now have been told I have only a short time to live before lung cancer claims me. Ironically the clear air, has served the cancer too. I am sure, doctor, you understand how this might be.'

'Yes, though little research has been done on it,' replied Mel.

'And once I knew this, I also knew that this meant that you, Soṉā, would soon be here, in time to meet with me again before I die.'

'But surely there is much you can do?' I said, alarmed by his words. 'You mustn't die.'

He laughed gently.

'Apparently we all must. Is that not so, doctor?'

'There is no shortage of research about that. But how has the diagnosis been reached and what treatment recommended?'

'I had to go to Kathmandu which I would never wish to repeat. I had some sort of scan in a noisy tube using magnets.'

'That's an accurate description of what is known as an MRI, Magnetic resonance imaging.'

'The doctor said that I had advanced metastatic cancer in my right lung and that there were signs that it had spread through the lymph system to my bowel. He didn't really think there was any treatment that would not be worse than the illness, and I accepted what he said and returned home. Dying well is an art I am striving to acquire and so, for as long as possible I will maintain my practice. And so, dear Soṇā and Mel, this is why you are here, to come before I die.

'I am feeling overwhelmed,' I said. 'First Elise had to die, and now you. What does this mean?'

'It means first of all that you have your very own psychiatrist travelling with you,' Jampa said, laughing as he did. 'It also confirms, that you are doing the right thing to continue the work of singing the silent song, perhaps begun here long ago, and which you heard in the long retreat, but which you then recognised and followed to your Elise. But she too had to die, as I must, but you will not be alone which is why Mel is here, not just as a friend tagging along, but herself hearing the first notes of the song and knowing she must also learn to sing. Is that not right, Mel?'

'I would willingly stay here and care for you, Jampa, if you were to ask. But you are right. The first notes came to Lizzie here, and it has taken a long time for her now to be the bearer of that song, but I am serious about being willing to remain. I don't carry medication around with me, but I could do it. I was able to be there for both my parents, and I beg you to ask the abbot if I can come back here when Lizzie returns to England and be your doctor.'

'Oh goodness,' I said, '*Karuṇā*'.

'Yes,' said Jampa, '*Künshi* and *Karuṇā*, goodness and compassion, and I have no idea how I should respond.'

'Nor me,' I said feeling utterly bewildered.

'Your tasks are already allotted, dearest Soṇā, and possibly bringing Mel has been one of them. I must go now and talk to the abbot if you wish to hold to your offer.'

'Yes, I do, but not just to be here to care for you, but also to be here and able to learn how to enter into that pathway that my dear Lizzie has brought me to.'

Jampa stood and then reached out and took my hand.

'My dearest sister, you must continue in the way before you, but seeing you again before I die is wonderful beyond words. My remembrance of you has always been with thanksgiving.'

'Thank you,' I said, tears now overflowing from my eyes.'

'You mustn't weep for me, you should be rejoicing. I must now go but you and I can speak again, Mel.'

A Professor and a Doctor!

Elise had once quoted to me some words of the Danish philosopher Kierkegaard: "Life can only be understood backwards, but it must be lived forwards", and they never seemed more appropriate to me than now. The abbot had met with Mel, Jampa and myself, and agreed that she could come and live at the monastery to care for Jampa, and share in their life in so far as it was possible. She said that she would need first to get to a hospital as there were some supplies she would need, and he agreed that she and I should go and collect all she would need and then return.

We met the Abbot in his own room, and I couldn't help noticing that in the corner of his room in a tiny alcove there was a candle alight. *Shekinah?*

'Mel,' I asked, as we returned to the dormitory where unfortunately there were now two others with whom we must share. 'What are you thinking? You have a super job back home and yet you're committing yourself to something quite open-ended. You don't know just how long this will last.'

'Soṇā, what are you thinking?' she replied. 'You had a super Sangha and a great abbot, and you left for an open-ended commitment that even brought you back here?'

I was open-mouthed and speechless.

'I need to go and see the results of his scans, but if his primary lung tumours metastasise, it is likely that he will become very poorly. I will need to get some medication to help and support pain and so on. And I need to stay here, and that's your fault for bringing me.'

'In which case I am reminded of a very old gentleman who as I helped him to his car as he was leaving Samye Ling, responded to my "Take care, Donald", with "No, Soṇā, take risks!". What more can I say?'

I didn't know what to think even into the night as I tried to fall asleep. Just what did Jampa mean about my tasks having already been given? And it was Mel who asked to come with me, not me asking her, but I still couldn't answer her point about my own change of life. Yes, I had done so, and was this now the moment for her? And then, I thought of how it had been that our lives intersected? Was all that intended, and if so by...? I couldn't finish the sentence in my mind.

We left after meditation and breakfast on the following day. It was a two-bus journey to Dhulikhel Hospital in Kathmandu and it took most of the morning and Mel said we should find a hotel to give her time to visit the oncology department. I set off to do that whilst she entered the hospital with a conviction I'm far from sure was justified, but she seemed to know what she was doing.

In January and even with totally basic Nepalese I managed to find us a room in a nearby 2-star hotel. It was not going to be luxury but we were only going to be there for one night, so I paid up and then made my way to the hospital to wait for Mel.

The hospital was a modern building and seemed well-served with staff. At the reception I said I was waiting for Dr Rivers who had gone to see the Oncology Department.

'Ah,' said the lady at the desk, 'Professor Rivers (!) has been taken to the Kathmandu Cancer Centre. I assume you are her assistant, Dr McKenzie.'

'Er, yes (!).'

'I have instructions to call a car for you to take you to Hotel City Gaon, which I know you will find most satisfactory, and she says she will join you after seeing something of the excellent work being done at the brand-new facility.'

I decided to accept the hospitality of a car and did not return to the hotel I had discovered earlier and instead found myself in the relative luxury of a modern vehicle being taken in towards the city, and dropped off without my having to pay at a hotel which was certainly an improvement on my earlier attempt.

Entering the hotel, I was greeted with a "Welcome, Doctor McKenzie, allow me to take your bags to your suite (!). We are so pleased Professor Rivers has come from England to treat one of the monks at Namobuddha Monastery. I gather she is a leading expert in her field.'

'Leading,' I echoed, not wanting to say too much.

'Professor Swari with whom she is visiting has arranged for her to be brought here after her visit, and we hope you will both enjoy an evening meal here in our restaurant.'

'Wonderful,' I said, still largely speechless.

The suite to which I was shown was a sheer delight with air conditioning.

'I assume you have left most of your bags and equipment at the monastery but if you lack something, please inform us and we will provide.'

'Thank you,' I said, as the receptionist closed the door, leaving me in an absolute haze of wonder as to what it was to be a doctor!

There were two beds in the room, one a luxury double and a much plainer single. I supposed the professor should have the double, but until she returned, I would stretch out and rest.

The phone woke me in the dark and at first, I had no idea where I was and what was happening. I picked up the phone.

'Dr McKenzie,' said the man's voice, 'we have just been notified that Professor Rivers will be arriving in about ten minutes. I imagine she will be expecting you to greet her.'

'You imagine correctly,' I said, 'I am coming now.'

The "professor" would get the warmest of welcomes from her "assistant" I decided, completely over the top, betokening her exalted position even over a simple doctor!

The car swept in and out stepped Mel, a young man carrying a small case for her, which she hadn't had in the morning and which I assumed carried what she would clearly be needing for Jampa.

'Welcome Professor Rivers,' said the receptionist as she approached her, and this was backed up by other staff doing all in their powers to greet so celebrated a visitor. I was regarded as a second division medic now. It was almost like watching Basil Fawlty fawning over the psychiatrist! Once in the room I turned towards Mel and attempted a curtsey.

'Congratulations on your Chair,' I said, 'What are you now professor of and which university do you grace?' I couldn't resist a giggle.

'Professor of getting what I need from a new Nepalese Cancer Clinic. I quickly realised it would be the only way. When they heard the word at the hospital earlier, I was whisked away by magic carpet. I looked at brand new equipment and made all the right noises, dug deep into my memory about oncology and engaged in intelligent conversation before stating that I was here in Nepal on a mercy mission and urged their assistance. Nothing was too much trouble and I have arrived here with all I might need to care for Jampa who has been at the fore of my mind throughout.'

'I hadn't known acquiring a degree in medicine was quite so easy. Wait 'til I tell Tan that I'm ready to see patients!'

'Yeah, well I hope Buddhists are allowed to exaggerate in order to do good.'

I noted that she was in effect claiming to be a Buddhist but said nothing.

'Well, your reward is a good meal this evening – I've seen the menu – but we'll have to arm wrestle to see who gets the luxury double I've slept on all afternoon.'

'Oh, I've always been good at arm wrestling.'

'Mel, on this day I can no longer believe a word you say. You can have the double; you've deserved a night of luxury; it might be your last for some time.'

To our further amazement, Professor Rivers and Dr McKenzie, were provided with car and driver to take us all the way back not just to Dhulikei but to the monastery itself, the only slight fly in the ointment for Mel being a message passed on from the head doctor at the Cancer Clinic that he would come and see her at work with the patient.

'Hey, don't worry. I really am a doctor, you know, and I can bluff my way through almost anything,' she said as we watched the car drive away.'

'Not my problem, Professor,' I said with a wide grin, turning and beginning to walk towards the guests' dormitory, when we heard a voice.

'Dr Rivers,' said a young monk. 'The Abbot has prepared a room for you, so I will lead you there.' Mel turned and stuck her tongue out at me, as I walked, feigning lugubriousness as I made my way to the dormitory which now contained a group of four loud American women, if I can be excused the tautology!

I stayed until after lunch on the following day, allowing me a last meeting with Jampa, as well as time with Mel, to whom I gave the news that I had decided to return home on the following day having been able to use the facilities of the monastery's computer.

'But that means you're cutting short your holiday and that you won't get to Kanchenjunga.'

'I spent enough time alone yesterday to realise I don't want to be here by myself. I'm missing my family, and it seems my work here is done.'

'Oh, Lizzie, I'm sorry – this is my fault.'

'It's no one's fault. Everything seems to have fallen properly into place and I cannot but be glad. I have seen Jampa again which was always the real intention of the holiday. We were able to get to Hilepani and see my friend Hanka and some of those I taught who now have children in the same school. I will always have a mental Kanchenjunga to rely on. And you are discovering something wholly outside your safety zones, though what it will mean if and when you return, we must wait and see.'

'I think you mean when.'

I smiled as enigmatically as I could.

I was able to be alone with Jampa for just 15 minutes and even within the short time we had been here I could see he was weaker.

'Mel has told me something about Elise and her recent death. Can it possibly true she was both Jewish and Catholic?'

'She discovered she was Jewish when she was at university but did not know either, that she had been baptised when just three days old by the Catholic priest, who later became a hermit and many years later told her he had been waiting for her to return to him, much as you said you were expecting me.'

'You know as well as I that communication patterns among humans are even more complex than the internet. That is why you left your monastery to prepare for Elise's death. Is that not so?'

'I'm beginning to know just how little I know.'

'Knowledge is not power, Soṇā, despite what the scientists and politicians may tell you. I would suggest that it was in the days of your long retreat that in learning to throw off knowledge lay the discovery of the power to do what was right on the night you encountered *Karuṇā* in its fullest manifestation possible.'

'Gosh, Mel has told you a great deal, but you are correct and now I have seen it again in the instant decision she made to remain with you. But Jampa, I am not returning to Samye Ling. I could no longer survive all those people coming asking question after question or just playing out their adolescent western Buddhist fantasies. I will return to my new home and my new family and just wait.'

'In which case my work is done here, and I can die, with the assistance of my doctor, at peace, having completed that which I was waiting to do which is to add my blessing to you.'

'I owe so much to you, Jampa, or I do to that young Australian-Nepalese called Brett.'

'He and I thank you for the privilege of being enabled to pass on to you something special. Now you must leave me.'

'I shan't forget you.'

'And I shan't ever leave you, Lizzie.'

I had my final lunch sitting with Mel.

'Hey, I said, pointing to the bowl before me, 'dhal.'

'Plus ça change, plus c'est la même chose.'

'Maybe it always will be. Can I ask what if anything you need me to communicate to your workplace? Don't forget you have a car in our car park and a house in Teesdale.'

'I apologise about the car and I have here the keys for you to move it somewhere if need be. I don't think I shall be here long, but hopefully long enough.'

'Explain, please.

'Jampa says he's been holding everything together until you arrived and now he can admit just how poorly he feels. I can help him as death draws near. It won't be long though. Meanwhile my inner life is undergoing some sort of change which is going to require considerable adaptation when I return, and a considerable amount of help and support from you.'

The first of my two buses to Kathmandu left in the early afternoon and I would probably be at the airport by 9:00 pm so I decided I would just sleep in the terminal building in readiness for my early flight via Abu Dhabi. Mel waited with me until the bus arrived and we hugged and kissed.

'See you,' were her last words to me, and I wondered why she might have omitted the word "soon".

Back Home

I knew I was back in the UK when I discovered there was a train strike, meaning that I had the choice of waiting in London for a day or getting the overnight coach from Victoria Station which would get me to Bedale around midnight. I decided to telephone Pieter from the airport.

'Is there any chance I might get a vet attend an exhausted human animal at about midnight at Bedale Bus Station?'

'Lizzie? Are you being serious? Where are you calling from?'

'Victoria Coach Station in London. I've managed to get a seat on the overnight to Edinburgh which calls in at Bedale. There's a train strike

'Just you?'

'It's a long story, Pieter.'

'Save it. Of course I'll be there.'

I had lost all sense of the days of the week and found out from a kind person on the bus that it was in fact Friday evening. That meant I had been away just twelve days instead of the three weeks I had planned, but sitting on the relatively supreme comfort seat of the coach north I was able to sleep most of the way and had to be awakened by a fellow passenger to whom I had informed my intention to leave at Bedale.

It was not in fact the bus station but the motel adjacent to the A1 allowing passengers a comfort break. Waiting near the steps was a grinning Pieter.

'I didn't think it would be the bus station, so I waited until I saw the coach turn off the main road and followed it in here.'

I gave him a huge hug.

'Welcome back to Yorkshire,' he said.

'Words that are music to my ears.'

As we drove home up towards the Dales, I endeavoured to explain that Mel had encountered a medical emergency for which she would be remaining in Nepal, and that I therefore had decided to cut short my time away.'

'That's such a pity.'

'Actually, Pieter, it was enough, and besides which I was beginning to miss my family.'

'You might not get the chance to lie in when morning comes, as I more than suspect Julia will come in and wake you up as she goes out to milk the goats, and Gale soon after.'

'And how is mama?'

'I think Elise's death has affected her considerably. She seems to have less energy.'

'Pieter, she's in her 80s.'

'Yes, I forget that, but I do know she is so looking forward to porridge with you in the morning.'

'Fiene's porridge! I've been dreaming about it. If I never eat curried lentils again it will be too soon.'

He laughed, and soon we were back in the familiar town I loved, and in the house I loved, and best of all, in the bed I loved!

Having come and sat on my bed earlier with Julia, Gale had disappeared off to school to play in a hockey match for the Senior team even though she was still only 14, getting a lift with the mother of one of her fellow team members. Julia had finished milking and was now working in the small dairy with Raj.

At breakfast over porridge, I told Fiene and Pieter the whole story of my visit and how I had become a doctor for a day, which amused them greatly.

'Though Mel is a real doctor, isn't she?'

'Yes, though clinical work was a long time ago, but I could see Jampa trusts her and that is half the battle. I am just adjusting my mind to try and make sense of what has happened.'

'Do you think Mel will return?'

'I don't know. I could see the possibility that in a country where there are good medical facilities in the city but nothing much outside them, she could build a life working with poor local people and even continuing to live at the monastery, but I just have no idea, and according to Jampa that was how it was meant to be.'

'Elise said to me that things were chosen for her, and that implied a chooser,' said Pieter, 'and I could follow that but then she would never allow any talk about the sort of chooser any of us might think of, even and perhaps especially those of her Jewish religion. I am still baffled but I accepted what she said, mainly because she just got on with whatever she had to get on with and said no more.'

'I feel the same,' added Fiene. 'Though it helped that we both loved her and could see the qualities she brought from silence into the world.'

'And if Jampa was right when he said I was meant to bring Mel to him, it kind of implies I was meant to come to be with Elise here and with you. And as a Buddhist, of course I do not accept any sort of god, and then I saw Elise in action and things changed. I still don't accept the existence of almost anything that can be described or spoken of, and yet, and yet, I know *Shekinah*, the Presence.'

'Do you know, Lizzie, I think you are not meant to know and even speaking to us is perhaps going beyond what you should, and certainly beyond what you can do,' said Fiene. 'The only person who will truly understand you is Gale.'

Pieter looked at me and gently nodded.

'Yes. Grace has always been very clever and will make a great vet, discovering her Judaism as she does so. Julia is already looking towards farming and agricultural college. Both have inherited much from their mother. Gale seems to have inherited something quite other, and the astonishing thing is that like Elise she does not seem to need to talk about it.'

'I've been aware of that for a while but for me the best part of Gale is that she can live with that and still be a perfectly normal 14-year-old and something of a wizard and thug on the hockey field.'

We laughed.

Raj texted his mum when Julia had told him I was back, and it didn't take long for Aishe to appear.

'Where's Mel? Her car's still here. What happened?' she asked.

'I became a doctor for a day, and I lost a psychiatrist in a monastery! Just a normal sort of holiday.'

Aishe laughed and over coffee in the sitting room I told her the story of our visit. As I concluded she stared me full in the face and I looked at her beautiful eyes, and said, 'Do *you* think it was meant to be?'

'Yes, totally, but how and why I cannot know. Of course there are coincidences in life, but I did not know Jampa was dying, and Mel thought she was going on a holiday in Nepal to broaden her mind. Well, she's doing that certainly. I was astonished how hooked she became on the Tibetan singing and the meditation that followed. When I was on remand at her Unit, she once asked me if I had become a nun because I was in love with Jampa, and for that matter whether I was in love with Elise, and I answered yes but not possessive love. Now I think she too is in love with Jampa and if she does return home, it might even be as a card-carrying

Buddhist.'

'You hadn't foreseen that possibility? After all she must have been heavily influenced by your conversations with her to invite you to stay in her home and then drive you here. Is it not possible that the person she is in love with is you, and that all she is doing for Jampa and becoming a Buddhist, is because of the love she has for you.'

'I'd never even considered that possibility, but it might make sense, I suppose. But now tell me about you, Tan and Raj.'

'Raj has become a goat farmer and is working closely with Julia! It's wonderful really, because they've known each other as best friends since infant school. I keep having to remind him of the forthcoming GCSEs but mostly he only reads books about goats, and he's also wondering whether he and Julia shouldn't try to buy some sheep too.'

'Ah, but can they afford the vet's bills?' I asked with a laugh.

'I blame Elise,' said Aishe.

'Yes, and mostly so do I.'

When Gale returned from hockey, after scoring a goal, but still losing and almost being sent off for repeated foul play, she came upstairs to my room and sat with me overlooking the valley. I told her about my trip, and she roared with laughter that I had been a doctor for a day but was fascinated about Mel staying behind to care for Jampa.

'Lizzie, was it mum who suggested you went to Nepal?'

'I think it was my initial idea but she certainly urged to set it up, and even when she knew she was dying, she made me promise to go.'

'Then it *was* meant. But what are you going to do now? Please don't go away again.'

'I have no plans for anything and especially for anything that would take me away from here. I shall continue to work in the surgery but want to redouble my practice and continue teaching meditation to any who ask.'

'Could you teach me?'

'I'm far from sure, Gale, you need to be taught anything. I think you already know a great deal.'

'But I need to learn to enter the silence and you are the only one who can do that for me.'

'But I only know it in a Buddhist context just as your mum knew it as a Jew and a bit Catholic.'

She smiled.

'Well, I am a Jew, as she was, so how about Jewish with a bit Buddhist.'

'I know you're serious, so the answer of course is yes though dirty fouls on the opposition are supposed to be unacceptable!'

'What about punching teachers?' she asked with a wide grin. 'You *do* know it wasn't a coincidence that you met mum and then came here, don't you?'

'Gale,' I said, 'go away!'

She gave me a huge smile and left.

It was now well past the time when Mel and I had been due back from Nepal. I had heard nothing from her, but nor it seemed had Christy at the Unit near Barnard Castle, as she explained when she managed to reach me on the surgery phone number, at a time when I was working.

'Hello, the Veterinary Surgery.'

'Can I speak, please, to Elizabeth McKenzie?'

'That is me.'

'This is Dr Christy Wyn from the BPD Unit. I'm calling to try and find out what might have caused my colleague, Dr Rivers, to be delayed on her holiday in Nepal, but as you are back, I imagine she must be too.'

'I can't tell you when she will be back, and I rather assumed she would be making contact with you. When I left, she was staying in a monastery south-east of Kathmandu, looking after one of the monks who is dying of cancer.'

'What?'

'Yes, and I think you should assume that if she comes back, it will only be after the monk for whom she is providing end of life care has died. She thought it would not be too long before that happened, but as with you I have received no word.'

'What on earth do you means by *if* she comes back?'

'To be honest, I'm not totally sure myself what I mean, but I still think that it's an if rather than a when. Her car is still in our surgery car park and I can see it from where I'm talking to you. I can only assume that she will be in touch with you though I don't think you will be able to contact her very easily, and by now it's more than possible that she is also working as a kind of doctor to the local community.'

'What has possibly brought this on other than your influence on her which I know was considerable during your time here?'

'I went with her as a fellow tourist, two people on a holiday and for me it was the chance to catch up with a couple of people I knew when I was there for a year before university. She said she wanted experiences outside the comfort zone of her brain. Perhaps those experiences have had an impact on her.'

'Well, it's having quite an effect on the work that we are able to do here. I wonder if her new experiences have enabled her to forget those here in need of her skills and energy?'

'I don't know the answer to your questions. I am hoping, as no doubt you too, to hear something. If I do, and she wishes me to let you know, of course I will do so at once.'

She rang off, clearly cross, to say the least, and of course I could see she had a point, but neither was I ever going to be critical of one who had shown such *Künshi* and *Karuṇā*, as Jampa had correctly described them and followed where they pointed.

A Visit to Nidderdale

Two days after the phone call from Christy, my mum rang to say that a letter for me had arrived from Samye Ling asking that it be forwarded to me. I asked her to open it and read it.

'It says,

"*Dear Bahuputtika Soṇā, my daughter, peace be with you. I have received a message from the Abbot of Namobuddha Monastery in Nepal. It said that we should regard you now as a mendicant, but still attached to the monastery here, as it is clear that living out the dharma is central to your life. The letter said you have shown great compassion in enabling one of the monks to receive the best of treatments as he draws close to his death by bringing a doctor, who has now herself taken refuge and is serving the medical needs of the local community from her base at the monastery. So I am full of joy in every way other than that we miss you here, and I am allowing the suggestion you be allowed to be a mendicant of Samye Ling, we hope you will also come back to us.*"

'Thank you, mum. Can you forward it to me, please?'

'Is he referring to Mel, your doctor at the Unit?'

'Yes. She's still there and possibly Jampa has not yet died, which of course he might have done had his life not been prolonged by her care. Those she worked with here will not be as delighted as I am to hear the news. And I think it quite possible she will not return. Her mum and dad have died and to the best of my knowledge, other than those with whom she works she has no family ties, and the perspectives of her existence have been turned upside down, or perhaps I mean they have now been turned the right way up.'

'Oh, Lizzie, you do seem to have quite an effect on those around you.'

'So it would seem, though I do wish they would stop dying.'

Having received this news, I decided to telephone the Unit and speak to Christy. The receptionist said she was with a resident but would call me back, which she did half an hour later.

'I have some news about Mel,' I said. 'It is not from her, but a letter sent to me by one who had heard from the monastery where she is caring for a dying monk. It says that in addition to her end-of-life care for the monk, she is also serving the medical needs of the local community from her base in the monastery.'

'This is frankly bizarre, and I really don't know what it is you have done to her. We have still heard nothing and I'm beginning to wonder of we shouldn't be asking the British High Commissioner to look into this. She works for the British government and has commitments here she is not fulfilling.'

'I can't imagine anything would follow from that. She is acting under no duress. If I had thought that was the case, I would have sought help from the Commission in Kathmandu myself. And the letter also said she had "taken refuge" which means she has made a commitment as a Buddhist.'

'Oh my giddy aunt! Do you think this means she won't actually return?'

'Not at all. She can be a Buddhist and do the work she was doing, and she has a house in Barnard Castle and a car parked here in the surgery car park. I can't see how she could possibly not come back, frustrating as it must be for you and your team.'

'Nevertheless when someone employed by the government fails to return from a foreign holiday there is a protocol I must follow.'

'Yes, I can see that. But unless she chooses otherwise, it's clear she's seeking to do as a doctor what she can for those who are benefitting from her. The medical services in the city are good but almost non-existent where she is. You know her very much better than me, so what do you think she might do?'

'I have known her longer but more recently you have been the lodestar she has followed.'

'She asked if she could accompany me on holiday back to where I spent a gap year when I was 17. Once she arrived at the monastery and met the dying monk she was guided only by her own concerns, not mine. The planned itinerary of my holiday fell apart, and I decided to come home. She did not follow me then.'

I had no sense of guilt about it but was totally confused. I decided that possibly the best thing I could do would be to suggest to Aishe that she and I drive via Masham into Nidderdale and talk it over with Leah. In every way she was nearest to Elise and perhaps she could help me sort my thinking out, though I had a strong sense that Elise, had she been here, would have told me just to stop thinking and live!

Aishe was more than willing to come and the drive into Nidderdale where I had not been before was easy and in pleasant countryside throughout. Masham is famous for its brewery, though lost on us, as neither of us drink!

Pateley Bridge is a tiny town at the top of Nidderdale but sits in the valley near the river. Leah and Ursula had lived here for many years now and were clearly a well-known part of the community, as when we went for a walk, just about everyone we passed spoke to them by name with a warm greeting. Clearly the Nidderdale synagogue of two was well-respected, and doubled in size when Leah's daughters came to visit. Ursula had worked in Harrogate as a solicitor before retiring but still gave pro bono advice to various people in the town.

Leah laughed when I told her the story of my visit to Nepal and how I had lost my former jailer cum psychiatrist. I also told her the latest news from Grace in Liverpool and her gradual integration into the Reform Community, as well as recounting how Julia was gradually expanding her farming empire together with Raj.

'It's a wonderful story,' said Aishe. 'From his first day at school Raj became close friends with Julia, and the occasional squabble apart which these days is about the breed of sheep they want, they have remained so very close.'

'Yes, I've seen them together when I've been over, and it's a superb partnership they have,' said Leah. 'And what of Gale?'

'We all know,' I said, 'if we open our eyes that Julia is almost the spitting image of her mother. Pieter told me he almost called her Elise one day, so strong is the likeness. But Gale is the one who is so very close to what I can only call the heart or soul of Elise. She now makes sure that she sits in the room with candle burning for at least 20 minutes before she has to get the bus to school. And only yesterday she came home to say she has a trial for the North Yorkshire Under 16's hockey team about which she's totally delighted though only this morning before she left the room, she told me that sitting in the room each morning, and I'm far from sure what she means by it, lies at the centre of her life.'

'It's quite fascinating. In Tanakh, before Elijah is taken up, Elisha asks a double portion of the Spirit of Elijah be given him. It seems to me that the spirit of Elise (a name with a similar Hebrew source to Elijah and Elisha, El being one of the names in Tanakh of *HaShem*) has divided her Spirit into three. Grace is already growing into the Judaism that Elise did at her age living with a family as her mother did with us; Julia has received that passionate love for dairy animals that Elise embodied; and Gale?

Well, it's hard to say exactly what it is, but I suspect we all know without being able to say exactly, just as her mum could not or would not say more than was absolutely necessary to anyone.'

'Who was Elijah? I've never heard of him,' said Aishe and I said the same.

'Elijah was a prophet who disturbed the peace of false religion and fled from Jezebel into the isolation of the wilderness where he discovered the voice of *HaShem* not in earthquake, wind or fire, but in the almost silence of a tiny breeze.'

'What a story,' I said. 'Mind you I think Gale intends doling out earthquake, wind and fire against her opponents on the hockey field.'

We all laughed.

'Her sports teacher told Pieter that he thinks she's very good indeed and certain to be selected.'

'But that's marvellous,' added Ursula, 'because it makes her more like Elise than ever, that unusual capacity given to very few of being utterly and completely amongst people and things with that hidden iron spiritual discipline that she doesn't need to talk about.'

'The only thing, however, is that I'm altogether sure what spirit Elise has left on me. I'm just totally confused,' I said.

'You understand a great deal, Lizzie, a very great deal,' said Aishe, 'and of the four of us you have most closely drawn near Elise in the experience of your own solitary years on Holy Isle. And if we are honest, your account of losing your friend in Nepal fits exactly in line with Elise's encouraging you to go. How you managed to pick up Mel en route via your days in prison would have amused her enormously, but not even remotely surprised her. And it should not surprise you either. Jampa was the turning point of your own coming to Buddhism. Try telling us it was just a coincidence that Mel chose to stay with him as he approached death!'

'I know it wasn't. Nor have any of my involvements with the woman whom I first met as the wife of a vet been anything even remotely approaching coincidence, but that's why I'm so confused. It doesn't fit my Buddhist theory.'

'Well, if that's just your problem,' said Leah, 'then it seems to me it's as it should be. That's why you're not Soṇā at Samye Ling, because you had the courage to live in the present no matter how uncomfortable and demanding than with the dead weight of the past.'

'But I'm assuming, and of course I'm not an expert in these things,' continued Leah, 'that your problem is the one faced long ago by Pieter when he first met Elise. She knew that the circumstances of her life, and those with whom she became closely involved implied a chooser. Deeply rooted in the Talmud from her time in Jerusalem and teaching rabbinic students, she took the word *Shekinah* to speak of this if she absolutely had to, which as you know was rare. She never defined it, and if anyone rejected the possibility she would not argue, because she knew there was no point. That refusal, not merely reluctance, to say even to Peter and Fiene more than the minimum about there being a chooser, won them to her. But Lizzie, don't tell me you don't know what I'm talking about, because you know I do, and I know you do.'

'Yes,' I said somewhat miserably. 'I think returning to the origins of my Buddhist life has somewhat thrown my balance.'

'Thank goodness for that,' said Aishe hastily, 'I thought it was just me that had my presuppositions turned upside down by Elise, not once but over and over.'

'Excuse me saying this to you three,' said Ursula, 'because I know you are much more advanced in these matters than me but isn't that how we advance in most of the important things in our human story. My rabbi once said that history was a gradual unfolding of truths, not a once and for all delivery.'

'In all my contacts with you, Ursula, which have not been as many as I might have wished,' I replied, 'I have never found you anything other than an unswerving repository of wisdom. Thank you.'

A Driving Test

We need our wits about us as we drive. Road traffic accidents still account for many deaths each year, not least among the young, and yet sometimes it is possible to be lost in thought and driving mechanically – certainly not recommended - but usually not in our immediate control.

As we returned from Pateley Bridge, Aishe and I continued the conversation which demanded a great deal of concentration and could quite easily have led us into trouble were it not the fact that the roads we had chosen were largely traffic free and that there were two of us looking where we were going.

'I know Elise would not, nor as Leah said, could not speak about *Shekinah*,' said Aishe, 'but are you really as confused as you said, Lizzie, or is a part of you feigning confusion to avoid something you don't wish to see?'

We had reached a part of the road that narrowed considerably, and I applied my mind to this, which was a useful way of not having immediately to answer Aishe's question.

'I'm not suggesting for one moment,' added Aishe, 'that you are deliberately putting on a false display, but our minds can do funny things, not least concealing from our conscious mind insights and truths that lie deeper and that are uncomfortable to face. I'm pretty sure that's one of the tenets of psychotherapeutic theory and practice.'

'H'm,' I replied.

'And if it so, Lizzie,' she continued, 'then perhaps I am doing the same, but perhaps inside you there is a battle which should perhaps be dealt with before you once again begin your Buddhist meditation group, encouraging others, including Gale who will want to join the group, in something you have actually been forced to leave behind.'

'Tell me about you,' I said, 'and perhaps it will encourage me to face what may possibly be happening within myself.'

'In entering into my Hindu heritage at an advanced age, by which I mean I was not brought up nor taught Hindu thinking and practice, I have been brought face to face with a multiplicity of myths and more deities than can be imagined. When I spoke with Elise about how disconcerting this was, she told me to concentrate on meditation and to regard the stories and myths as the many faces of the One. But like all claims of divinities, I began to think I must pray to this One, and do what religious people do everywhere, and treat it like an oracle hoping to influence it on our behalf. But this seemed ridiculous when I thought about it, even though I knew Elise had *Shekinah* at the heart of her own life and practice. I wanted to speak of this to her when she became ill and there was no opportunity. So, Lizzie, tell me what you think is going on.'

'To the best of my knowledge, most people who claim some form of belief in a deity, whichever it might be and however sophisticated their thinking, in the end regard it as a sort of local or personal deity. Indeed, evangelical Christians encourage belief in a personal god though they are always falling out among themselves and starting their own denominations because the personal god is usually no more than a projection of their own inner needs, which include the will to power, as Nietzsche described it.

'I became a Buddhist and learned all about how gods were manipulations by humans and best left completely behind in our thinking about the meaning of our lives and those of our fellow human beings. But there was always a hint somewhere that beyond that which we can speak of there may, just may, be that which cannot be spoken of but nevertheless is.

'I gave this no thought as encouraged by the Buddha not to waste our lives doing so and there can be no question that this is true. Libraries across the world are full of books which are nothing more than intense speculation about their own mental constructs, sometimes known as theology. At a practical level these ideas quite easily take the form of idols, both mental and physical, whole communities, nations and even empires built upon them. They are like a chimera manipulated by our needs and used by those in power to maintain their positions, often supporting them with grander and grander titles from vicar to Pope and all stations en route.

'Yeshua taught that no one should be called teacher, rabbi or father, and yet the churches that claim to follow him have created a veritable panoply of titles with which to adorn themselves. It is the same in other religious traditions, including my own. Poor old Yeshua, after his death he became Lord and Messiah, the Christ, totally ignoring all he had taught.

'But that is not how it is with *Shekinah*. Presence is simply that, and not more as we might wish. I've been reading the *Diary of Etty Hillesum*, which Elise was reading at the time her illness began. That young woman entered the concentration camp at Auschwitz with the constant awareness of Presence but not imagining this would prevent the deaths of millions of her fellow Jews, including her parents and herself. It wasn't her who wrote the words but some other unknown Jew awaiting gassing, but she would have endorsed the words:

"I believe in the sun

even when it is not shining
And I believe in love,
even when there's no one there.
And I believe in God,
even when He is silent.'"

'I understand this,' said Aishe, 'and I can see how it makes even more sense of our silent meditation.'

'Yes, we don't have to create idols, including those erected by our own multiplicity of words. Silence seems to be the métier chosen by *Shekinah* but to imagine that therefore there is nothing is to be completely mistaken, as I would bear witness from my long retreat and even more by Elise's five years of silence. There is a song, but it is silent, and can only be heard in silence.'

'Oh, Lizzie, you're not even remotely confused, but one of the things I have been reading and reflecting upon, by Abhishiktananda who was also the Catholic priest Henri le Saux is that the Presence external to ourselves has to become the Presence within.'

'Yes. And those in whom this takes place we commonly call mystics, even though I think there are far fewer than we might imagine. Etty perhaps was one, but Elise was a stricter Jew and would always eschew the possibility of union with *Shekinah* and maintained that Yeshua as a Jew would never have claimed to be one with *HaShem*. There is a saying, I think from Zen Buddhism, that if you meet the Buddha on the road, you are to kill him, the implication being that anyone who claims anything wonderful for themselves is by definition a charlatan. The true mark of holiness is familiarity with suffering.'

'When I was studying,' said Aishe, I knew an older lady who was convinced that the Indian guru Sai Baba was some sort of incarnation of the divine. She was an ordinary person who had previously had some contact with the Anglican Church in Wales, and yet in old age she threw herself into the life of a devotee of this man, who spoke of love and had done acts of kindness when he was young, but then as time went on, gathered around him tens of thousands of devotees. She even travelled and put up with terrible living conditions just to be near the man who arrived in an extremely expensive Bentley. Even then she could not see the charlatan beneath the skin and the oddest Afro haircut imaginable. But do you think we make an idol of Elise?'

We had stopped at a traffic light on red allowing oncoming vehicles to cross the bridge over the Ure, between Middleham and home.

'It's a good question. Jews are taught always to be on the lookout for idolatry in its varied forms. I loved Elise, but if you had been present with us that night in the heavy snow at Samye Ling, you would understand why I was so captivated by her. She manifested immediate *Karuṇā,* that compassion which is the end towards which Buddhists are aiming. Instinctively at various levels of my being, I knew I would have to come and be with her. But I hope I still do not make an idol of her. She made no claims, she did no miracles, answer prayers or speak in tongues, and in fact she spoke of these things mostly only to you and me, and I don't think we could describe ourselves as her devotees providing her with money in return for spiritual wisdom.'

The light had turned green, and we were almost there.

'Thank you, Aishe,' I said to my friend as I drove up the incline into town, 'your questions are of course also mine, and together we have begun to answer them.'

Lizzie arrived home to find Fiene unwell and in bed which was most unlike her. Pieter had called Tan and he came to the house to see her. From Pieter's description of her symptoms, Tan suggested that she may well have had what he called a TIA (Transient Ischaemic Attack), a sort of mini stroke. Tan knew Fiene would resist any attempt to move her to hospital and Pieter said his mum wished to remain at home whatever.'

Pieter had told the girls to leave Oma in peace this evening, but I wanted to sneak in for just a moment to see her.

'I wanted to come and see you, Fiene, to encourage you to do what will never come naturally to you, that is to rest and let the rest of us take the strain. For many years you have held this family together. You are the one who has always been present and, in every way, reliable. You even helped all of us through Elise's death and that must have taken an enormous amount out of you whilst living with a broken heart yourself.'

'Oh, Lizzie,' she replied quietly. 'I loved Elise so much, no one will ever know just how much. When we lost her my world came to an end. I know I have Pieter and the three girls, and now I have you, but she was my daughter, and my loss has been terrible.'

'I would guess that Tan, and we know he is a good doctor, was determined to speak of this in medical terms, but I have no doubts that what you are experiencing in your body are the terrible depths of loss and bereavement.'

'In a wonderful way the girls are manifesting in different ways the wonder that Elise was, and I am greatly consoled by that, and everyone remarks on how like her mother Julia is. But no matter what happens to me, I hope you will remain here because they are going to need you in ways I cannot foresee but feel certain about.'

'As long as Pieter wishes me to, I will stay here, Fiene, I promise. But now try and get some sleep and that rest the doctor ordered.'

I went down into the kitchen which was empty of the woman whose domain it had been for so many years but found Julia doing the cooking for the evening meal.

'I think mum would want me to be here,' she said, in a matter-of-fact sort of way.

'Yes, she would,' I said and then heard myself saying, 'I was in love with your mum.'

'You and most people. Dad used to say to me how lucky he was to be at the front of the queue, and they were so unbelievably happy together. Being called Julia was mum's idea, and dad has often said it was exactly typical of mum's generous nature to name me after his first wife and to keep her photograph up, still after all these years. It must have been truly awful for him, to lose his young wife after so short a time together, but he has told me often enough that the day he met mum helping test cows for TB with him, it was if the clouds had opened, and allowed the sun to shine again. Do you think we should have carrots with this?'

I almost burst into laughter at the total incongruity of her question after such a wonderful statement.

'Yes,' I said.

'Yes to carrots or to what else I was saying?'

'Yes to both,' I said with a broad grin. 'But do you know, Julia, you not only look like your mum and have her incredible generosity of heart, but something of your Oma rests on you too.'

'I shall never be able to cook like her.'

'Nobody could, but I think you'll grow into it.'

'Do you think she's going to die, Lizzie?'

'No, well not yet anyway. She's just in deep mourning and will need some time to recover, but she is an old lady, don't forget, and one day you and I will also be, so let's not expect more of her now than she can manage.'

'I know you said you loved mum, but I want you to know how much I love you, and how much Oma and dad, and Grace and Gale do too.'

'Well, I love you all too and I'm afraid you're stuck with me.'

Along the Banks of the Swale

Fiene gradually recovered strength over the next couple of weeks and now often worked in the kitchen with Julia helping.

A further month passed when one morning my phone rang and it was Mel. She was back in the country and making enquiry as to the whereabouts of her car which she had left in the surgery car park.

'Your car is still where you left it, Mel, and I have the keys you left here before we went to Nepal. But I'm more interested to know about you and Jampa. How are you and where are you?'

'I'm back at home. I came back last night and as yet have not made contact with Christy. In fact, she doesn't know I'm here.'

'What do you want to do about the car?'

'I think the easiest way would be for me to get a taxi and come when you will be available to meet with me so I can bring you up to date.'

'I would like that, Mel. I have been worried about you.'

'Yes, I should have been in contact but look, might you be about this afternoon. I'll try and book a cab to make sure I'll be with you by mid-afternoon.'

'Forget it, Mel. I'll come and collect you and it'll give us the chance to talk in the car. I've nothing on today. Fiene has been poorly but she's feeling better and can probably manage without me.

'Ok, but is there any chance you can get here in time for me to buy you lunch at the Tan Hill Inn? It will help remind me of the hills.'

'Of course. I'll get going as soon as possible.'

I arrived at her house, and it was clear she was looking out for me at the window and at once came out and got into the passenger seat, putting a rucksack on to the back seat. She leaned towards me and kissed my cheek.

'When you're ready,' she said hastily.

'Are you not wanting to be seen?' I asked, feeling a little confused by the haste with which she seemed to want to operate.

'It's complicated,' she replied, and obviously it was.

For the first few miles as I drove through Barnard Castle and on up to the A66, she said nothing. Finally, she said, 'Jampa died peacefully almost two weeks ago. One of the last things he said to me was about you, that our arrival at the monastery was because you had been brought back to see him before he died. He was buried on the day after he died, and I left immediately afterwards much to the dismay of the other monks and those who had been attending my primary clinic that I had established.'

She said no more until we reached Tan Hill Inn, the highest pub in England. I pulled in, we entered and ordered food and drink. I told her that Christy held me answerable for what had happened to her.

'If anyone is responsible, it is the man who turned your life upside down many years ago when he was just Brett, an Australian Nepalese, who then became Jampa. I kept vigil with him throughout his final days and hours. He spoke to me gently, fitting for one with the name meaning "Gentle Voice".

'He told me he first became aware of your presence during the meditation on your first morning there, by the sheer quality of your silence, and at this time you were not the Buddhist practitioner of meditation you later became. He said that one of the talents with which he seemed to have been blessed was the ability to hear silence, and from you he said, there was a wonderful silent song.'

She paused as our food arrived.

'He also told me that he knew on first meeting and when you returned a couple of months later that your coming to the monastery was not some kind of accident as it might be for the tourists, and that he knew from that day to the one in which we turned up, many years on, that you would be returning before he died. Hence, when he knew he was dying, he was waiting for you to come soon, and you came.

'Your return was not unaccompanied, however, and I was able to provide the right sort of end-of-life care he would not otherwise have received. By careful use of analgesia in the form of diamorphine I was able to relieve his pain almost completely without sending him to sleep constantly. In the sort of words the Hospice Movement in the UK might have used, he died a good death, gently slipping away, his breathing becoming shallower.

'Word had got round that there was a doctor there, so in addition to my time with Jampa I was sought out by those living in the area, though to be honest there was little I could offer them without medication, but I did what I could. So, the day after Jampa died and not waiting for his funeral I left and decided to travel east. I took advantage of your friend Hanka in Hilepani with whom I stayed for two nights to plan the rest of my itinerary.

I knew there was one place I had to visit, and it required long and typically tortuous bus rides and crossing the border into India, but eventually without any real scrapes I made my way to Darjeeling, and then north to Gangtok. You know why.'

'To see Kanchenjunga.'

'I did it for you, Lizzie, because I know how much you had wanted to see it again, and that because of me you had lost the chance. And what can I say? Truly it is a holy mountain. I would have liked to trek to Tingvong Monastery to be even nearer but was warned off by local guides who said they didn't accept women even as tourists but even from Gangtok the mountain is a wonder, and there was an occasion very early one morning when I was due to travel back to Darjeeling, that I stood there and I thought of you and all that Jampa had said about you and I sobbed.'

By now I was crying and took hold of Mel's hand tightly.

'Thank you.'

'I travelled south of Darjeeling to Bagdogra Airport where I took a flight back to Kathmandu (from which flight the views up towards the Himalayas were astounding), and from there a flight to Heathrow. Yesterday I took the train to Darlington and a taxi home, though I'm far from sure it is home anymore.'

'I take it no one at the Unit knows you are back.'

'No.'

'And how long before you let Christy know.'

'Perhaps that depends on the nature of our conversation.'

I was taken aback.

'I'm not sure what you are saying. Are you implying you may not go back to work?'

'When I was a junior doctor, I had to work in A&E some of the time. Occasionally people would be brought in following horrendous accidents with injuries that we quite rightly described as "life changing". Patients lost limbs or suffered brain damage, or perhaps came in following a stroke. These were life changing.

'My time at the monastery with Jampa did not in itself have that effect. It was what he told me about you, followed by my visit to Kanchenjunga. These have been life-changing for me, Lizzie.'

I could not speak for a while.

'Let's pay our bill and get off. We can talk in the car.'

Tan Hill Inn is at the apex of a triangle of roads, both running towards Swaledale, one via Stonesdale on to Keld and Muker, by the banks of the Swale, where it meets the other road that comes down via Arkengarthdale. I decided to take the former, perhaps unconsciously wanting to follow the course of a river as we had done in Nepal.

Stonesdale is not quite mountainous Nepal, but its own beauty cannot be denied and for most of the time I drove in low gear to make the most of the scenery. At one point we had to stop when we encountered a herd of sheep advancing towards us, which we both enjoyed. I recognised the farmer as someone who occasionally collected drugs from the surgery but on this occasion his attention was given wholly to the sheep and his dogs, and he didn't see me. At the bottom of the hill, we turned left onto the cross-Pennine Road between Swaledale and Kirkby Stephen in Cumbria. In winter it was often impassable because of snow.

We had not yet spoken since leaving the inn, so I began.

'I did have some news about you.'

'Really? How?'

'After I left you at the monastery the Abbot emailed my own former Abbot at Samye Ling, and he in turn wrote to my parents and they rang me. The mention of you was secondary to what he wanted to communicate about me, that I should be regarded as still sound and living the dharma faithfully, which was at least news to me. He said that you were staying to care for Jampa and had acquired many locals coming for medical help. He also said that you had "taken refuge", which means that you had become a Buddhist.'

'What?' She sounded shocked. 'Lizzie, that's not the case. I have done no such thing.'

'I did think it unlikely. Buddhism is a matter of becoming, not just signing on a dotted line, and it can take a long time. On the other hand, just before I left, you had become a Professor, feted across Nepal, so anything might have been possible!'

She laughed, the first time she had since I had picked her up, which I thought good news. Someone once noted that someone in a passion cannot laugh, and that once there is laughter the passion is dissipated. There was certainly some energy within Mel, but I was relieved that it had not turned to passion.

'Whilst I was in Darjeeling, before travelling north to the holy mountain, I met up with three young Indian women in the hostel and we travelled north together. They were lively and we laughed a great deal, but I was impressed by the serious nature of their pilgrimage for that is what they were, pilgrims seeking understanding and clarity about their lives and life itself. Even in the dormitory with me present they engaged in simple rituals and a period of silent meditation. When faced with Kanchenjunga I glimpsed in them your face as you had looked upon the holy mountain. It was not just with awe, and many of the tourists certainly experienced that, but was also with wonder. For them it was above all the spiritual significance of the mountain that had taken them, and I believe they were richly rewarded by the experience. And that was the defining moment for me. Ever since Jampa had spoken to me about you, I had known I wanted to get back to you but now, I began to understand why and what it was that was drawing me. Dare I say that in that moment I experienced, however fleeting, Presence, what your Elise called *Shekinah*?'

We were passing through Gunnerside Gill, in the heart of the former lead-mining part of the middle Dale.

'And did you do anything else interesting on your holiday, doctor,' I said.

We both laughed, knowing instinctively that we were engaged in something serious, but which must not become solemn.

I continued up the rise out of the village and soon we were entering Reeth, where I found somewhere to park on the village green. There were groups of walkers completing their treks and sitting by open cars removing their boots and refreshing themselves with tea from their flasks.

'So, Mel, what now?'

'You'll think what I'm going to say is crackers...' she began.

'As opposed to all you've just told me,' I interrupted with a grin. She responded with a broad smile.

'When I got back from the mountain to Bagdogra Airport and waiting for my flight to be called, I recalled a song from my youth, a song by the Beatle, George Harrison, "The Art of Dying". It's actually a very noisy piece of rock music but I kept going over and over the words in my mind.'

'You'll have to tell me. I'm much too young to know it.'

"There'll come a time when all of us must leave here
Then nothing sister Mary can do
Will keep me here with you
As nothing in this life that I've been trying
Could equal or surpass the art of dying
Do you believe me?

There'll come a time when all your hopes are fading
   When things that seemed so very plain
   Become an awful pain
   Searching for the truth among the lying
   And answered when you've learned the art of dying.
   Do you believe me?"'

I found myself unable to speak for at least two minutes. Eventually I took her hand in mine.

'Right, I said, let's get going.'

I drove through Grinton and up the steep roadway over the top into Wensleydale and home.

Homeward Bound

There was a full house when we arrived back. The girls were back from school, Pieter from doing things to pigs best not recounted, and Fiene, who was looking stronger than after her TIA, as Tan continued to describe it, of course baking.

'Hello everyone. Mel already knows Pieter and Fiene, but this is Julia who farms goats assisted by Raj, and this is Gale, the terror of the hockey pitches.'

'Hello, Lizzie has told me lots about you and I'm so delighted to meet you.'

'You stayed behind in Nepal when Lizzie came home?' asked Julia.

'Yes, and I got back just last night, and I fear it's my car that's been taking up space in the surgery car park.'

'That's where we held our special event after mum died,' said Gale.

'And I met Lizzie when she was sent to the naughty step after her punch-up defending the good name of your mum. And if Lizzie has talked to me about you, she has spoken even more about your mum, and I so wish I could have known her.'

'Thank you for saying that, Mel,' said Pieter. 'And I love the idea of Lizzie being sent to the naughty step.'

Everyone laughed at me, which I greatly enjoyed.

'Mel's going to stay. She doesn't fancy driving home in the dark. Is that ok?'

'She can have Grace's room and a choice of beds,' said Fiene, but first a mug of tea and a piece of my cake.'

'I hoped you might say that,' said Mel.

That evening it was not possible for further conversation but when I entered Elise's room early next morning, I found the candle had already been lit by Gale, and there alongside her, sitting upright but relaxed with her eyes closed, was Mel. Gale left after 20 minutes to get ready for school but then there was a great noise from upstairs and we heard someone running down and into the room where we were still sitting. It was Peiter.

'Mel, please can you come? It's mama. There's something wrong.'

Mel quickly followed Pieter up to Fiene's room, and slowly I followed, where I found the two girls and Pieter standing around the bed and Mel sitting on the bed next to Fiene. It was clear from the way Mel was attending to her that Fiene was dying. She wiped her brow and gentled rubbed her hand, and I saw her whispering something close to Fiene's ear and I saw Fiene's eyebrow make a tiny move almost in response.

After that I'm sure we could all see that her breathing was getting slower and softer, but then she mouthed a word to Mel, who now encouraged Pieter and the girls to come to Fiene and be there holding her hands, she herself now stepping back. Within five more minutes Fiene had very quietly slipped away.

Mel did and said nothing but allowed Pieter, Julia and Gale to just be there with their beloved Oma and mama. It was Julia who asked Mel what it was she had said to Fiene.

'I said, "Fiene, it's okay now, you are safe to go.'

'But didn't she try to say something to you.'

'Yes. She said just one word. It was difficult for me to catch it, but I'm pretty sure the word was "Elise".

Julia and Pieter were now crying, but Gale looked at me and gave me a smile and I gently nodded my head.

In turn we all approached and kissed Fiene for the last time. I thought just how much I loved this woman, and then for some reason I began gently to sing the same gentle Scottish ballad I had sung with the two parents of the baby baptised by Elise.

The others looked up at me but allowed me to continue though the effect was to bring more tears to the eyes of us all.

'That was so beautiful, Lizzie,' said Pieter. 'Thank you so much.'

'I loved this woman, as we all did. In so many ways she has been the heart and soul of our family, never seeking to be other than there for the others in her life, welcoming and caring for those who came as visitors or close friends in exactly the same way of complete self-giving we also knew in Elise. That was the song sung after the tiny baby baptised by Elise up in Scotland after he had died.'

It struck me as I looked at the face of Fiene that already it was relaxing, that her life has shown forth the reality of *Karuṇā*. And then suddenly it was my turn to weep. I, as well as her family, had lost Elise and Fiene in a matter of six months. Mel put her arm round me and drew me to her, and in that moment, I redoubled my determination to remain here and support them as best I could, as I know Fiene, and Elise herself, would have wanted.

'The cause of her death was readiness,' said Mel to us all, gently and kindly, 'in that the time had come when she was ready. I cannot write that on a death certificate but that is what it was. As we weep, we do so only for ourselves, but we need not weep for your Oma and your mama. I am sure of that.'

'Thank you for being here with us, Mel,' said Pieter.

'Yes,' said Julia, whilst Gale gave Mel a smile.

'Pieter, can you call Fiene's GP, and let him know there was a doctor present, so he needn't rush, but you can say that in medical terms it was heart failure, also known as readiness. But I'm not her GP and he will need to sign the certificate.'

Eventually we all gathered in the kitchen, and already Julia was at work preparing the porridge Fiene would no longer make for us. As we finished, Gale gave me a nod in the direction of Elise's room and as the others were getting the dishwasher loaded and Peter was on the phone, I joined her.

'This is why you brought Mel, isn't it?' she said. 'To be here to allow Oma to die? And in her last moment, she was aware of mum, wasn't she?'

'Gale, my darling, what can I say? You don't need me to tell you that Mel came all the way back from Nepal yesterday to be here this morning. You know that and I do, and I think Mel does too. I cannot possibly know what Fiene knew in that last moment, but I cannot think of any better name to be on my lips as I die than that of your mum.'

Inevitably we now both burst into tears and held one another.

Through the tears, she said, 'Lizzie, I think Mel is meant to stay.'

'Yes, I know that too, but are you going to tell her or shall I?'

We wiped away the tears as we both gently laughed.

Bizarrely, but typically, after Pieter had phoned Grace and then the doctor's surgery, there came a phone call for him on the surgery line, where as yet no one would have been in. A dog had been hit by a car in Carperby and was being brought in at once. Pieter had no choice but to head straight for the surgery, yelling to Julia to call Willa and get her to come at once. Gale telephoned school to let them know that neither she nor Julia would be in today and explained why. She then followed up Pieter's call to Grace and they spoke for some time.

Mel and I sat in the sitting room with its wonderful view down to the River Ute and the hill rising above, and suddenly I had the thought that Mel and I should drive up to the gallops at Middleham onto Elise's favourite place.

'I shouldn't really be here,' Mel said. 'Bereavement and loss are primarily for the family.'

'Do you know, Mel, for someone so very intelligent you are remarkably stupid. Why do you think you are here? Come on, get some shoes on and a coat. We're going for a walk.'

This morning there were horses galloping up and down, a fascinating sight in itself, but we made our way on the safe side of the white fencing to Elsie's picnic place, where we sat down on the grass.

'Now, 'I said, 'the time has come for you and me to make some decisions.'

'Surely you'll be staying. They need you.'

'I didn't mean decisions about me. They have been made already. No, I mean the missing Dr Melissa Rivers who used to work at the BPD Unit in County Durham.'

'"Used to work"?'

'That proved you were listening. Yes. I can't know what you were thinking in the long hours of the night, but it must have included a recognition that there is no way that you will be returning to Barnard Castle other than to sell your house.'

'Were you listening at the door by any chance?' she said with a smile.

'And I hope that by now, even into your scientific mind which of course, as I know from all our conversations, would quite rightly reject all talk of things that were "meant to be" in terms derived from any sort of god-talk, you will now realise that for reasons none of us know, some things are meant to be. You were meant to go with me to help Jampa out of this world, and you arrived back yesterday to come here to do the same for Fiene.'

'Fiene needed no help from me.'

'Oh, she did, Mel. You saw how well she was yesterday. Your

arrival meant that now she could go.'

'This is all very bewildering.'

'I should hope so, and that's how it's meant to be, my wonderful friend and companion.

'All I knew was that I had to come back to you.'

'And thank you, Jampa, for that, allowing you time even to visit Kanchenjunga for me as well as you, and who knows, one day we might get another opportunity to visit together, but for now having been sent here, I think you must remain.'

'But I can't just billet myself on a family I hardly know.'

'I am certain that sometime today, Gale will want to talk to you and insist that you are meant to stay. She will tell Pieter and Julia and they will agree. Besides which you are special to them. You were here when Oma left us. You were the last to speak to her and the one who heard that very special last word. You are now family. I realise that there are practicalities to be sorted, to do with the Unit, your house and so on, but this is where you now live, with us. You are part of Elise's family.'

'Well, yes, I think I had realised that when Jampa was dying and now it has been confirmed this morning.'

We left the gallops and returned home. Tan had called and confirmed Mel's diagnosis of coronary thrombosis. The undertaker had called and taken Fiene's body, but choosing a time for a funeral and what sort of funeral needed to wait for Grace's return from university for what would be the Easter and Passover holiday.

As she had said to me much earlier that morning, Gale spoke to Mel and told her that the family would welcome her staying with them if that is what she wished, but that she, Gale, also knew that Mel had been here for a reason, and should stay, where she could, along with herself, grow into singing the Silent Song, first heard by Elise herself and then Lizzie.

'"You do know it can't be spoken of without it no longer being the Song", she had told Mel, who in turn told Gale about her visit to Nepal, that the monk Jampa had told her she needed to stay close to Lizzie.'

Gale came to see me in my room.

'I have asked Mel to remain here, and she says she will, possibly looking for part-time work locally, possibly as a community psychiatrist. Dad and Julia agreed, and we have decided that she should have Oma's room as her own. I so hope though, the funeral will have to be fitted round my match for the Under 16s; I've been chosen.'

I smiled. She had indeed been chosen. For Gale the reality of both *Shekinah* and the rest of her life integrated seamlessly. I knew it was my task to lead and teach both Mel and her, the way into meditation, but ever to be prepared to recognise that there would come a day when Gale would be the true successor to her mother in singing the Silent Song.

Printed in Great Britain
by Amazon

16062919-6a79-4b78-b668-8f390d1ed732R01